A small velve[t]
and into her li[...]

She smiled at it. She had wondered when Roger was going to give it to her. She had seen him pull it out of his dresser drawer. She had also seen him tuck an envelope into the same drawer, but then they left for Manny's and there was no time to question his actions. Her gaze met his.

"Happy anniversary." Roger's jet black hair had just enough wave in it to give it a little body, and his dark eyebrows almost shadowed his eyes, giving him an air of mystique and danger.

She could hardly believe it had been a whole year. They'd had a few rocky times as any normal couple would, but overall it was a great year. "I love it."

He chuckled. "How do you know? You haven't even opened it."

"I love it because it's from you."

MARY DAVIS is a full-time writer whose first published novel was *Newlywed Games*. She enjoys going into schools and talking to kids about writing. Mary lives near Colorado's Rocky Mountains with her husband, three children, and six pets.

Books by Mary Davis

HEARTSONG PRESENTS
HP399—Cinda's Surprise
HP436—Marty's Ride

Don't miss out on any of our super romances. Write to us at the following address for information on our newest releases and club membership.

Heartsong Presents Readers' Service
PO Box 721
Uhrichsville, OH 44683

Or visit www.heartsongpresents.com

Roger's Return

Mary Davis

Heartsong Presents

With much love to my dad, Art Greig.
And to Kristen Heitzmann and Doug Hirt.
Thanks for all your help!

A note from the author:
I love to hear from my readers! You may correspond with me by writing:

Mary Davis
Author Relations
PO Box 719
Uhrichsville, OH 44683

ISBN 1-58660-628-X

ROGER'S RETURN

Cover illustration by Jocelyne Bouchard.

PRINTED IN THE U.S.A.

one

A small velvet box slid across Jackie's menu and into her line of sight. She smiled at it. She had wondered when Roger was going to give it to her. She had seen him pull it out of his dresser drawer. She had also seen him tuck an envelope into the same drawer, but then they left for Manny's and there was no time to question his actions. Her gaze met his.

"Happy anniversary." Roger's jet black hair had just enough wave in it to give it a little body, and his dark eyebrows almost shadowed his eyes, giving him an air of mystique and danger.

She could hardly believe it had been a whole year. They'd had a few rocky times as any normal couple would, but overall it was a great year. "I love it."

He chuckled. "How do you know? You haven't even opened it."

"I love it because it's from you."

He shook his head with a playful smile. "Just open it."

She eagerly did as he commanded. First the red ribbon. Then she tilted the lid up. She lifted out a delicate gold chain, and from it hung a gold cross with an inset diamond. "It's beautiful!"

Roger came around behind her and took the necklace. She scooped her hair out of the way. His warm hands brushed her neck several times as he seemed to have difficulty getting it clasped. "There." He caressed her neck with a gentle kiss.

Ten thousand volts of electricity shot through her. She took a deep breath. Maybe they should skip dinner and head back home.

As Roger was returning to his chair, the waiter came to ask

if they were ready to order yet. Roger requested another minute and raised his menu to scan the dinner selections.

She fingered the cross. Should she tell him about his gift now? It would be eight months or so before she could give it to him, but she could tell him now.

"Roger." She folded her menu.

"Yes, my love." His gray eyes peeked over the top of his menu. "Have you decided what you want?"

"No," was the only breathless word she could manage. Roger could have been a leading man thirty feet tall on the cinema screen. At times it was still hard to believe he was hers. All hers.

Her parents had had reservations about him, but they had been wrong. Roger doted on her. When his loving gaze lit on her, it still sent her heart racing and a thrill coursing through her. Sometimes, like now, it made her feel like the first time he told her he loved her and she realized she loved him too.

"I'm due for some time off, maybe in a month or two." He leaned over the table closer to her. "I was hoping I could get it for our anniversary, but the timing was off. What do you say to a drive down the coast, find a cozy little bed and breakfast, and hide out for a week or so, just the two of us?" His gaze pierced hers, and her heart went into double time.

"Roger, really! Can you really get it off? Oh, I'd love it."

Their waiter stood by the table, his pen poised. "Are you ready to order?"

Roger ordered steak, and Jackie ordered the grilled salmon. After the waiter left, she thought she would tell him now, but his gaze took her breath away. Too good to be true. She had everything she wanted right here, a loving husband and a baby on the way. *Thank You, Lord.*

The beginning of a smile tipped the corners of Roger's mouth. "I could sit here all night and feast my eyes on you."

His intense gaze sucked away not only her breath but her

thoughts as well. What was she going to tell him? That's right, her surprise. She opened her mouth to speak while she still knew what she wanted to say, but the hostess handed Roger a slip of paper.

Roger raised his index finger. "Hold that thought." He pulled his cell phone from his jacket pocket and pressed the on button. "I just need to make a quick call."

Grr. How she hated that thing. He had turned it off so they could have the evening to themselves. He would turn it on for only two people, her and his boss. She folded her arms across her chest and mouthed, "Mr. Moore is a control freak." And she would tell him so if she ever met the man. She didn't even know the man's first name. Roger referred to him only as Moore. He was as elusive as Roger's job description.

She couldn't make any sense out of the one side of the conversation, but she could tell from Roger's tone their anniversary dinner was about to come to an abrupt end. Mr. "I want" Moore always called Roger away from her. Not this time! Not today! Not on their anniversary! Roger would have to make his boss understand that tonight was off limits. He could have Roger all day tomorrow. He had turned the phone off for a reason.

Roger slipped the phone back into his pocket, his gaze averted. When he finally raised his gray eyes to her, the regret in them confirmed it. "I promise to make this up to you."

"Not tonight!"

"I wouldn't if I didn't absolutely have to."

Just once she would like for him to tell Moore no. A big fat NO!

"If things go well tonight, we can take that trip sooner."

Okay. She would wait until then to tell him her surprise.

"Please don't be mad at me. I have no choice." He came over to her chair and kissed her before leaving. "Moore's picking me up. I'll be home as soon as I can."

She wanted to grab him and keep him there but instead let

him go, choosing to focus on their upcoming romantic get-away. When their dinners arrived, she stared at the food the waiter placed before her. The aroma accosted her senses, and she willed herself not to get sick. She tried to breathe as little as possible and then only through her mouth. As their waiter passed by the table, she flagged him down. "Could I get boxes for these—and the check?"

"The gentleman already took care of the bill. I'll be right back with those boxes."

She packed up the food and left.

The apartment was dark and quiet. Wasn't this the perfect anniversary, with Roger abandoning her for work and her feeling like throwing up? But there was nothing in her stomach.

She replaced the napkin holder on the table with a pair of candles and arranged the restaurant food carefully on two plates. A quick zap in the microwave to warm the food, a little candlelight, and their anniversary wouldn't be a complete loss. She lay down on the couch to wait for Roger and pulled the afghan over her.

The next morning, she rolled off the couch and went to the bathroom, relieving her stomach of what little wasn't there. She peeked into their bedroom. The bed was still neatly made. Hadn't Roger come home at all last night? On their small dinette table sat their dinner, still waiting. Repulsed by the thought of food, she scraped it into the trash, grabbed a package of soda crackers and the phone, and curled up on the couch. Punching in the number for Roger's cell phone, she waited for him to pick up. She got the voice mail recording and left a message. That was odd. He always picked up, even if only to say he couldn't talk and would call back. Always. *Lord, please have Roger call back or, better yet, walk through the door.*

She would wait right here on the couch for Roger to return her call. She wrestled a soda cracker out of the package and nibbled a crumb off the corner.

When the phone rang later, Jackie jumped and snatched it up. "Hello!"

"Hi, it's Mom. Are you okay?"

"I'm fine. Why?"

"Well, you said you were coming over this morning."

That's right. She was going to tell her parents they were going to be grandparents after she told Roger last night. But she hadn't told Roger, and he should be told first.

"It's already eleven o'clock."

Was it really that late? And still no Roger. "I overslept."

"You're not sick, are you?"

Sick? Hardly. At least not in the way her mom thought. She wished she could be happy about this, but without Roger— "I'm fine, Mom, really. I'll come over another time."

After hanging up, she tried Roger's cell phone again but didn't leave a message this time. She paced from the living room to the dining area and back. Roger had never been gone this long before, and he would have called. What if he hadn't been gone long at all? What if he came in last night and saw her sleeping and didn't want to disturb her, then left again this morning before she woke? That must be it. But why wasn't he answering his cell phone? She had to believe he was safe and in God's hands. *Lord, please be with Roger right now and let him be all right.*

When it came time for her to go to work, she called the hospital to let them know she wouldn't make it in that night. Her nausea was better, but only if she lay motionless. Her morning sickness had hit hard and fast. She drifted in and out of sleep, dreaming of Roger sneaking up to her and kissing her on the cheek, but she was never able to wake herself to see him. She tried to talk or scream or move, to do something, but she was paralyzed. She finally woke dazed in the early evening. Brewing herself a cup of tea, she dialed Roger's cell phone again.

Instead of being greeted by Roger's full, deep voice, a

thin, hollow one came over the line. "Hello."

She froze, her breath trapped in her lungs.

"Hello? Is anybody there?"

Could this be the elusive Mr. Moore, who had taken Roger away from her last night? "Who is this?" she demanded.

The man hesitated. "Detective Ford of the Seattle Police Department. Who is this?"

Seattle? But she lived miles away in Issaquah. "I must have dialed wrong."

"Ma'am, wait! I'd like to talk to you."

"I didn't mean to call the police department."

"You didn't. This cell phone was found and turned in to us. We've been trying to find out who it belongs to."

Found? "It's my husband's phone. He'll be glad to get it back. It's practically a growth on the side of his head. Where was it found?"

"Down on the waterfront. Could you come down to the station?"

Jackie jumped into her car and drove straight to the station, praying for Roger the whole way. She stepped into Detective Ford's office and took the offered seat. He was on the phone, a man in his fifties with salt and pepper hair, heavy on the salt. He wore a green golf shirt with SPD monogrammed on it. His voice wasn't nearly as thin as it had sounded on the phone, but it still had the same resonant drone to it.

She crossed one knee over the other and wiggled her foot. She had expected to pick up Roger's phone at the front desk and be on her way. Her morning sickness wouldn't permit her to be up and around for long. She twisted her wedding ring round and round on her finger.

The detective smiled at her and raised his index finger, indicating he'd be with her in a moment. He put on his glasses and read something on his calendar, then told the person Friday was good and hung up. "I'm sorry to keep you waiting, Mrs.

Villeroy." He removed his glasses. "Thank you for coming down." He stood and reached across his desk.

She shook his outstretched hand. "They didn't have my husband's phone at the front desk and told me to come up here."

"I asked them to have you sent up to my office. We had a call into the manufacturer to trace the phone, but their computer system was down. Said they'd give us a call back as soon as it was up, but then you called. Could you wait just one more minute?" He walked around his desk to the door. "Sorenson, do you have that report?"

"Right here."

"Thanks." Detective Ford walked back around his desk with the file open, then sat down and closed the file. "Do you know where your husband is?"

"I'm not sure. He could be at home."

"Would you mind calling and seeing?" He pointed to the phone.

Jackie picked it up and dialed. The answering machine picked up at the apartment. Roger's vibrant, happy voice boomed through the line with her giggle in the background. She listened to the whole message before hanging up. "He's not there yet." She pulled her wedding ring off and on over her knuckle.

"When was the last time you saw your husband?"

That was a strange question. Her ring got caught on her knuckle. "Last night. But I'm sure he came home and just didn't wake me."

He gave her a conciliatory nod. "Do you know your husband's blood type?"

"Blood type? Why?"

Detective Ford didn't answer right away. He pulled a plastic bag from his desk drawer with a cell phone in it much like Roger's. He placed the bag on the side of his desk closest to her. "Does this look like your husband's phone?"

She swallowed hard. Why was Roger's phone in a plastic bag like. . .like evidence? "Yes." The single word caught in her throat.

"That's blood on your husband's phone."

Blood? Her hands began to shake, and her ring tumbled to the floor. The sick feeling in the pit of her stomach had nothing to do with morning sickness.

❧

Jackie hadn't gone into work all week, the phone her constant companion. It had been the most miserable week of her life waiting for any news about Roger. Then this morning, to have her waiting end in the morgue. *Lord, I can't take this. This is all too much.* She took a slow breath to calm her nerves and stomach before passing through the double doors of death. Her doctor had said her morning sickness would pass soon, and she would be able to eat normally again. Morning sickness? For her it was morning all day long. The smell of ammonia, formaldehyde, and other chemicals burned her nose and set her stomach boiling. She stopped and held her breath, willing her stomach to hold what little it had in it.

The police officer who was escorting her stopped as well. "Are you all right, Ma'am?"

Jackie nodded, trying to breathe only through her mouth, but she could still smell the nauseous odors. She placed her hand on her belly. Oh, why hadn't she told Roger about the baby?

"We can wait a minute if you like."

"It's just a little morning sickness." Being a nurse, she had seen dead bodies before. She had even been down in this morgue before. It wasn't the morgue or dead bodies. It was the combination of smells mixing with morning sickness and the strong potential that this dead body could be R—could be her— The blood type and basic description matched.

She had wanted her father to come with her but was unable to reach him at work. She could have called her mother, but her mother couldn't even handle the thought of the morgue. So Jackie was on her own.

She took a deep breath through her mouth. "I'm ready." The sooner she knew, the better. She stepped through the doorway and up to the steel gurney with someone draped in a sheet. *Oh, Roger!*

The morgue technician took hold of the edge of the sheet. "He's been in the water for a week, so his coloring is off, and he's bloated."

Jackie held up her hand to stop him. She needed one more moment before she officially became a widow. Once that sheet was pulled back, there was no more hope, and there would be one less John Doe in the world. *Lord, give me the strength to make it through this.*

She nodded. The technician pulled the sheet back slowly. She gasped at the swollen, waterlogged face and clasped her hand over her mouth. Staggering back, she bumped into the officer and turned toward him. She had been warned the body was ravaged.

He led her over to a chair, helping her into it. "I'm sorry, Ma'am. They just need your signature; then you can go."

Jackie shook her head and took a deep breath through her mouth. "It's not him."

"Ma'am? Am I to understand this is not your husband, Roger Villeroy?"

"Roger doesn't have a mole on his cheek." It really wasn't him. Hope soared, lifting her out of the morgue and into Roger's arms. But there was still this John Doe, and Roger was still missing. *Roger, where are you?* She wanted to feel his arms around her, not just the memory of them.

"Are you sure?"

She nodded. "May I go now?" She had a date with the commode.

two

Jackie pushed her son higher in the park swing. The higher RJ went, the more he giggled. A familiar creepy chill inched its way up her back. She had the strange feeling once again of someone watching her, observing her every move. She had felt that way two and a half years ago when Roger disappeared and so many times in between. Sometimes it was a comfort, as though someone were watching out for her like a guardian angel. Other times it terrified her. Today it wasn't the fearful feeling, but in either case she always wanted to be home away from prying eyes. Maybe if she had closure on Roger's disappearance, she wouldn't wonder if someone was there. . .if Roger was there.

She had prayed many times for Roger to come back to her. She'd reached the point where she thought the Lord might be telling her no to Roger's returning. Once she realized the Lord may not bring him back to her, it took three months before she could ask the Lord to reveal to her if he was indeed dead. She still felt she had no response and decided that meant she was to wait. So she waited, looking for his return. Then she would realize she couldn't continue to live in the past or spend so much time waiting on the future. She had RJ in the present she needed to focus on. So she vacillated between the past she had with Roger, the present with RJ, and the future dream of Roger's coming back. Would she ever come to terms with his mysterious absence? Why had she been selfish in keeping the knowledge of their child from him? Every time she thought of Roger, she regretted that single act.

Casually she glanced around the neighborhood playground. As always there were other moms with their children, some kids on bikes, and a pair of older boys tossing a Frisbee. There was more activity than usual in the middle of the day because of spring break, but no one out of the ordinary. Still, the eerie chill persisted, racing up and down her back, seeking a place to settle. She attempted to shake off the feeling with the argument it was just her overactive imagination and the puzzling disappearance of her husband.

Finally she couldn't stand the oppressive weight any longer. The urgency to flee overwhelmed her, no matter how inexplicable it may be. "Come on, Sweetie." She stopped the baby swing. "Time to go home."

"No! Go more." He kicked his legs, keeping her from lifting him out.

Lord, help me. RJ's feet caught on every part of the swing imaginable, and his hands clamped the chains with an iron grip. Once his feet were untangled and his hands pried off, she scolded him; but his tantrum continued.

"Me stay!"

"No, you go." She wrestled him into the umbrella stroller. He started to cry, loudly. The last thing she wanted was to draw extra attention to herself all the way home. Her nerves were already frayed.

She dug into the diaper bag. "You want some crackers?"

"No!"

"Some raisins?"

"No."

She dug deeper and came up with a solitary treasure. "I have a chocolate chip cookie." She knelt in front of him.

"Coo—kie." His crying stopped, and he reached out for the offered treat.

She ruffled his hair. "You've got your mommy right where you want her."

Chocolate from the cookie was smeared on his sweet little face. She tried to wipe it away, but instantly more replaced it. She squeezed his nose and kissed his forehead. She pushed toward home, across the grass and onto the path through a clump of maples and oaks. She paused at a fallen branch across the path and tossed it out of the way.

"Jackie."

She froze at the familiar voice. Could she be hearing things? She turned slowly and stared into a face she knew so well. Was she dreaming?

"Roger?" she asked faintly.

"Hello, Jackie."

He's alive! The excitement inside paralyzed her. She could only stare at him. Was he real? *Is this really happening, Lord? More than two and a half years.* If she moved, would the vision evaporate like fog in the sunlight? He looked so good, so much the same, yet different. There were tiny lines and a hardness around his steel gray eyes that hadn't been there before. But he was alive! *Thank You, Lord.*

Everything else faded. She saw only Roger. She felt herself sway, and he caught her. His strong arms enveloped her, and she leaned into him. "I can't believe it's really you."

He caressed her hair. "It's me."

She pulled back from him. "You're really okay."

"I'm fine." He smiled. "Better, now that I'm with you."

A question started to form in her mind, but then she realized—her suffering was over. Life could return to normal. And after all this time she could give him his surprise. She had always felt guilty not telling him that night. She turned to the stroller. "This is your son, RJ."

RJ had cookie crumbs and chocolate around his mouth and down the front of his shirt. "Oh, RJ." She reached into the diaper bag and pulled out a baby wipe.

"More, Mama."

"I don't have any more." She reached for his face with the wipe.

He craned his neck and head from side to side.

"It's okay," Roger said, squatting in front of the stroller.

She captured RJ's face and in one practiced swoop removed most of the cookie from his face. He scrunched up his face and shook his head.

Roger ruffled the boy's hair. "Hey, Kiddo."

RJ furrowed his brow and stared at his father.

She watched as Roger tried to get his son to respond to him. RJ only stared. He would warm up to his father in time. For now his father was only a face from pictures she had shown him. RJ was still young enough that when he grew up he wouldn't even remember his father hadn't been there for his first two years, except for the stories they would tell of Roger's absence to—

"Where were you?"

Roger remained focused on RJ when he spoke. "Away."

Away? She waited. There had to be more. After a few moments of silence, she realized he wasn't going to say anymore. "Away? What kind of answer is that?" She hadn't waited and suffered for two and a half years for some stupid vague answer.

"I can't talk about it now."

"Can't talk! You've got to be kidding! Then what are you doing here? I want to know what happened to you! The police found your cell phone. It had blood on it!"

He held out his hands and shook his head. "I can't."

This was too much to deal with now. She whirled around, pushing the stroller past him on the path. Suddenly all the strange things she had chosen to overlook—Roger's job, the vague evasive answers, his odd hours—crashed in on her. She had learned it was easier not to ask certain types of questions, questions about his job. His answers would be veiled, or he'd say he couldn't talk about it. The high-tech field was full of secrets, and its people were tight-lipped about saying much of anything. What was Roger's job really? She supposed there had been red flags, but she had chosen to ignore them. Now they were slapping her in the face.

"Jackie, please. I know I'm asking a lot of you, but I can't tell you now. You are better off not knowing."

"Better off," she said under her breath and turned on him. "If you can't tell me anything, then what's the point of this little reunion?" Tears streamed down her cheeks. "Why don't you just go? You've been dead to me for over two years anyway." She made an about-face, thrusting the stroller ahead of her.

Was she better off? What was Roger involved in that he felt he had to keep the truth from her? Did she really want to know? At least she didn't think he'd lied to her. She did have that. But how far could she push before he felt he needed to lie to appease her?

❧

He watched her retreat. *What did you think, Villeroy—that she would jump into your arms and all would be forgiven?* He had hoped. He wanted desperately to erase the last thirty-two months and hold her in his arms, never ever letting her go.

It hadn't gone as well as he'd hoped. But what could he expect? He was just glad she hadn't become hysterical. But then Jackie had never been the type. Always calm in the face of stress. After all she had been an ER nurse. Hysteria would never do there. But this was unlike any other stress she had faced, and he'd thought she might come a little more unglued. Her anger was justified, her pain still too fresh. He wished he had the words to soothe it. At least words he could tell her now. All he could tell her was to wait and to trust him.

He needed to trust too—trust God to help him work everything out, then show him how to regain Jackie's trust. He didn't know which hurt worse, having his beloved Jackie despise him or his son, his own flesh and blood, not know him at all. But the Lord would sustain him through this too, as He had the past two and a half years.

Jackie's angry stride took her quickly away from him. Her long brown hair swished back and forth from its perch on her head. He followed at a distance, knowing where she was headed, her parents' house.

If he had known a baby was on the way, he would have done things so differently. That night was supposed to have put an end to his troubles so he could live a normal life with Jackie. Instead everything went terribly wrong, and he felt he had no choice but to run and hide to keep her safe. *I'll make it all up to you, Jackie, if you'll let me.* He hoped her love was strong enough to get through this. He had to believe she still loved him, at least a little. He would put Jackie and RJ in God's hands and focus on what needed to be done.

❧

Jackie parked the stroller in her front yard. Her hands shook as she battled the strap that held her son. Finally she set him free and lifted him out, resting him on her left hip.

Roger was back! Wasn't that what she had prayed for? Or had she been hallucinating? No, it was no hallucination. Roger was real enough. She should have stayed back at the park. What if she had driven him away for good this time? But it was too sudden and too much to deal with in the middle of the park. *Away?*

She jerked the diaper bag free, and the stroller tipped over. She left it in the grass and fumbled for her keys. They clinked on the cement step of the front porch, and she scooped them up. Tears kept her from focusing on the right key. It was next to her car key. That one was easy to find. The keys tumbled to the ground again.

"Let me get that for you."

She gasped and stepped back.

Roger picked up the ring of keys and deftly slipped the right key into the lock.

"Why are you here? Why did you come back?" she asked, her voice a suffocated whisper.

"I had to." His words were tender and warm.

"Why now? Why not before?"

"I've come before."

"You were here and never got in touch with me? No word you were all right?"

"I couldn't, Jackie—believe me."

"Couldn't?" A tear slipped down her cheek. "Couldn't?"

"Mama cwy." RJ put a small sticky hand on each of Jackie's cheeks and turned her face toward him. "Mama sad."

She gave him a weak smile and rubbed his arm. "Mommy's okay."

"I'm sorry for startling you back there." There was a faint tremor in his voice.

She swung her gaze back to Roger and stared. Unsure what to think, she stepped inside, leaving the door ajar. She settled RJ in front of the TV and shoved *Willie the Operatic Whale* into the VCR.

Roger remained on the other side of the threshold holding the folded stroller like a trophy. "I think you need a degree to fold one of these things."

She took the stroller and laid it on the floor by the couch. She didn't know what to say. What to feel. She had tried for so long to feel nothing just to make it through each day, fearing she would lose control. She gazed at him. He looked the same in his black leather jacket and faded jeans. A spring breeze tousled his dark mane. He needed a trim. And a shave. This was just how he looked the first time she saw him in the ER, slightly unkempt.

"May I come in?"

She must have nodded, for he entered and closed the door behind him. She wanted to flee, to hide from the pain of his absence. At the same time, she wanted to run into his arms and let him soothe away the years. "Can I take your coat?"

"No, I'm fine." He snugged it closer.

"You want something to drink? A glass of water? Something to eat?" She tried to keep her voice from shaking. Why did she suddenly feel so nervous? This was Roger, for pity's sake—her husband. But she needed to do something, anything.

"No, thank you."

She scooted past him and into the kitchen. What had he come for? What would he tell her? Was he here to tell her good-bye? It would be more than she had last time. She pulled a glass from the cupboard and filled it at the sink, then held it out to him. "Sure?"

He shook his head. "I'm fine."

That makes only one of us. She raised the glass to her mouth, clanking it against her front tooth. She winced. He was fine. She took a drink. She hadn't been fine since the day he'd left. She poured the rest of the water in the sink and set the glass on the counter. She folded her arms, then unfolded them and stuffed her hands into the pockets of her tan shorts.

"You look good." A soft curve touched his lips.

"So do you." She turned back to the sink and filled the glass with water again.

Roger came up behind her and clasped her upper arms. "I've missed you."

She leaned back into him with a sigh. She had missed him too, desperately.

He slipped his hands down and rested them on her stomach. "I wish I had been there when you were pregnant."

That flared an anger she hadn't realized was brewing below the surface. She always wondered if Roger somehow knew she was pregnant and left because he wasn't ready to be a father. She took a slow, deep breath and turned around to face him, his arms still encircling her. "Why weren't you? And where have you been for two years, eight months, and two days?"

He let his hands fall away from her. "Ah, Jackie, don't do this."

"Don't do this! Don't do what? Don't remember every agonizing moment you were gone, wondering what happened to you? Don't remember my son's father abandoned me in a restaurant on our first wedding anniversary without a word? Don't remember the face of the man in the morgue the police hoped I could identify? Don't remember I almost lost RJ? Don't remember all the nights I cried myself to sleep?" She took a ragged breath, feeling her chin quiver. "What exactly is it you don't want me to do? I'm finally picking up the pieces of my shattered life, and you show up and scatter them about." She wanted to run away and cry, but she wouldn't give him the satisfaction of breaking down.

Answers—she needed answers!

"I'm sorry, Jackie. Truly I am—for everything."

"You're sorry! Is that all you have to say? Where did you go that night? Where have you been? A person doesn't just disappear for no reason. I deserve something more than 'I'm sorry, Jackie!' "

"You're right—you do. But I can't give it to you now." He held out his hands, offering an apology. "For the love you once had for me, please trust that my absence was necessary."

Secrets and trust don't mix. "Love? Is this one of those 'if you love me, you'll understand' issues? Well, I don't understand." She leaned back against the counter and folded her arms tight across her chest. "Enlighten me!"

He raked a hand through his hair. "You know I never would have left if I didn't have to."

"No, I don't know." She didn't know if she knew him at all—
or ever had. "Do you have some other wife, some family, I'll
learn about on TV?" She threw the words at him like stones.

"Don't be absurd. I love you."

She clenched her teeth. "What an interesting way to show it."

"My leaving had nothing to do with you. Don't you have
any trust in me left?" His brow furrowed.

"How can you ask me such a question—after what you've
put me through?"

He took a step forward, holding out his hands. "I need to
know you can still believe in me. I want to make it up to you."

She wanted to take a step back but was already up against
the counter, so she settled for shifting her position. "It's not
that easy."

"For our son then?"

He had done it, pushed the right button. When he disappeared, she was confused and afraid. In the moments
since he'd come back and had no answers for her, she'd
become angry and hurt. The wound lay open, hemorrhaging.
If she didn't gain control, it would sap away her life. At the
mention of their son, she felt a portion of her anger drain away.

"I love you, Jackie."

She stared at him again, caught in a vortex where time had
stopped. The past unchangeable. The future uncertain and full
of mistakes waiting to be made. Which mistakes could she
afford to make? Which could she avoid? Which would tear
them apart? She wished someone would tell her the right thing
to do. She stayed unmoved, not knowing what to do. They
both stood silent, some invisible line separating them, with
neither one willing to cross it. The singing whale crooned in
the background.

❧

"Mama, Mama!" RJ pushed between them, reaching for
Jackie. "Up."

Roger stepped back reluctantly. It was a short-lived answer to his prayer to hold his wife again. Too short.

Jackie scooped up RJ and held him close. "What's wrong, Honey?"

He snuggled up to her, a choke hold around her neck. Roger's longing to hold RJ grew. Jackie caressed the boy's dark hair, so much like his own. He wanted to touch it too.

"It's okay, Sweetheart. Mommy has you."

But not Daddy. He touched his son on the back, needing to make contact with his flesh and blood. "Hey, Kiddo."

RJ turned to him and pushed a hand against his chest. "No."

Jackie took an unsteady breath. "I think you should leave."

No, he didn't want to go. He wanted to stay forever. "May I take you to dinner tonight?"

"I don't think so." Hurt and longing—fear—uncertainty swirled in her chocolate eyes.

"We could talk."

"About what? The weather?" She shook her head in disgust. "I have to get ready for work."

"You still at the hospital?"

She nodded. "A different one."

"You always hated the three-to-eleven shift." Lame small talk to hang on to every second he could.

"It works out best for the baby-sitting." She caressed RJ's back and kissed his fuzzy head.

"I could watch RJ." He had missed so much already.

"Mom picks him up on her way home from work. That way he doesn't have to be at the sitter's long."

It was best if he stayed clear of his mother-in-law as long as possible. She had never approved of him; though civil, she'd always been cool. His leaden feet took him to the door. "I'll come back tomorrow." A promise he would keep if it killed him.

He walked back down the street toward the park, relishing

the memory of Jackie in his arms again. She had developed an inner strength at odds with her slender body. He was afraid she would need that strength before this was all over. There was a time when she never would have spoken crossly to him. He'd always sensed she feared losing him, that she didn't realize he was wrapped securely around her little finger, then as well as now. She was the only woman for him. Had he lost her for good? His stomach knotted. Jackie had gone to the morgue thinking he was there. *I'm so sorry for everything I put you through.*

He stopped at the swings and touched the one his son had been in, then stepped aside for a woman to put her child in it. He walked away with her glaring at him as if he were strange. He was just a father longing to be with his son.

Lord, he is so beautiful. Thank You for caring for him and protecting him and Jackie. I know I have to be patient, but I want them back. I want everything to be set right. If I had allowed myself to listen to You long ago, I wouldn't be in this mess, and we would be a family. Please make us a family again.

three

Jackie stepped out into the night air with two other RNs and took a deep breath. They always left the hospital in twos and threes to cross the parking lot in the dark. Her coworkers were having a discussion she was only half listening to about a particularly difficult doctor. She usually satisfied the doctor's wishes, but tonight he'd yelled at her for incompetence. Just the icing on the cake of a horrible day. Today had been a long week. Less than twelve hours ago, her life had been turned completely upside down. But then Roger had that effect.

She tuned back in when Dixie said good night to Ramona. Jackie and Dixie continued through the lot.

"Dr. Hoon was in rare form tonight. When he can't get along with you, I know he's having a bad day."

"It wasn't his fault." Jackie was normally the only one who could appease Dr. Hoon. She had figured out what he liked and could anticipate his requests. But not tonight. She hadn't connected one logical thought to the next. She had plenty of thoughts, just not related to one another. It had almost made her late for work. "It was mine. I'm having a very stressful day. I wasn't alert to his needs."

"I felt so sorry for you."

"As long as he doesn't bite, I can handle his bark."

Suddenly Dixie grabbed her arm and yanked her to a stop. "Let's go to my car. I'll drive you home."

Jackie's heart leapt at the sight of Roger, leaning carefree against the back of her minivan with his hands behind him. The lights in the parking lot cast a shadow across his face, making him appear more ominous, more mysterious, than

26

usual in contrast to his relaxed stance. Her wayward heart danced. Was she ready for this? She hadn't had time to think.

He had sent her thoughts spinning the night she met him in the ER; he'd rushed in carrying a sick boy he didn't even know. Roger to the rescue. Right place, right time, take charge. Despite her swirling thoughts, she had resisted the urge to fall for the handsome, mysterious hero. But he kept asking her out and finally wore her down. Once she agreed to go out with him, she fell easily in love. When she said "I do" six weeks later, it seemed as though she had known him much longer. And a year later, he was gone.

Dixie tugged on her arm. "Let's go."

Jackie remained unmoved. "It's all right."

"Do you know that guy?"

She thought she did—once. "It's okay. I'll see you tomorrow." Jackie forced her feet to move, pulled along by her heart.

Roger waited. "Did your friend warn you not to come over here?"

"Should she have?"

He pushed away from the van and pulled a bouquet of red roses from behind his back. "I won't hurt you."

But you have. She took the offered flowers, a disarming move. She should be ecstatic her husband was back from the grave. What was wrong with her? *Away. . .I can't talk about it.* Not even to his wife? "I'm not up for this."

"I just want to talk."

But not about his whereabouts the past two and a half years. "Tomorrow?"

Would she be any less confused then? "I don't know."

"I know we have things to work out between us, and I know they are all my fault. But I want a chance to work them out with you. Just a chance. That's all I'm asking for."

She knew the outcome if she gave him a chance. She would

be drawn to him beyond her control. He would gaze at her, and she would melt. But armed with that knowledge, she could resist. She unlocked her car door. But did she want to resist?

Like the gentleman he had always been with her, he opened her door. His arm lingered across the opening, hindering her from getting in. "In spite of everything, I still love you. I never stopped."

"I don't know you."

"How can you say that? We lived a year as husband and wife. You know me as well as anyone."

"The man I thought you were wouldn't have left without a word."

She ducked under his arm and slid into the driver's seat. He stood holding her door open but said nothing. She stared out over the steering wheel. She had been so excited to see him after all this time, and in one little word, *away,* he had taken her happiness from her. She knew she should get past it and move on, but she didn't want to. Roger had been fine, he said, and chose not to come back to her. She wanted him to suffer as she had. She was only human.

"It's late. I need to go."

He still said nothing. She would wait him out. He was reluctant to let her go, but he would, of that she was sure.

"I want to see my son."

His words were soft and undemanding. He must know that if he made demands of her she would shut him out. Maybe she did know him a little after all. And he knew her. She looked up at him. She couldn't deny her son the opportunity to get to know his father.

"Ten tomorrow."

"Thank you." He swung the door shut and stepped back.

❧

Jackie crept in through the garage door of her parents' house. The dim light of the TV flickered from the living room. Someone had waited up for her. She walked softly so as not to wake anyone else and tapped her dad on the shoulder from behind the couch. "You didn't have to wait up."

He patted her hand as he turned. "I can't sleep when your mother's not in bed."

"Where's Mom?"

"She crawled in bed with RJ. He was fussy and wouldn't stay in bed. He wanted you."

"I'm sorry." She heard the creak of the basement steps.

Her mother joined them. "I thought that was you. You're home a bit later than usual."

"How is he?"

"He's quiet now, but I don't expect it to last long. I'm not sure if it's just bad dreams or if he might be developing an ear infection."

"Thanks, Mom."

"Who are the flowers from? A doctor?" The hope in her mother's voice was unmistakable.

Her stomach knotted. She should tell them. They deserved to know. She took a deep breath. "They're from Roger."

Her mother looked as shocked as she herself had felt earlier in the day. "Roger? Your husband? He's alive?"

"Where is he?" her dad asked, his eyes widening.

She knew her parents would have questions. She had questions. But so far she hadn't received many answers. This one, at least, she could answer.

"In town."

"Where has he been? What happened?" her dad asked.

Here were the questions she couldn't answer. "I don't know. He hasn't told me anything."

"What do you mean? Why not?" her mother snapped.

"I don't know."

"For a woman whose husband has just come back from the dead, you don't know very much. And you certainly don't look happy," her mother said sharply.

Was she? Of course she was happy, but confused and angry he wasn't being honest with her. Right now that was what loomed before her.

"I told you there was something about him."

"Mother, please." Her mother had always said there was something about him she didn't trust. And Roger was proving her right. "I don't want to talk about it now. I just thought you should know."

She turned and headed for the basement, her sanctuary. It was almost like having her own place: two bedrooms—one for her, the other for RJ—and the recreation room. It held a mini refrigerator, microwave, hot plate, and toaster oven, with a small table and chairs for dining, and a couch and TV. Except for doing their laundry, she had to go upstairs only to enter and exit. But sometimes she lived as much upstairs as down. She didn't like the closed in feeling of the basement.

From the top of the stairs, Jackie could hear RJ crying. She had known he was upset when she left him at the sitter's earlier in the day. He had been clingy, sensing the tension between her and Roger, and she was too rushed to settle him before leaving. She hurried to his room and scooped him up, needing to hold him as much as he needed to be held. "It's okay, Sweety. Mommy's here."

She kicked off her shoes and crawled into bed with him. He snuggled up close and drifted off to sleep. Jackie wished she could fall asleep so fast but knew she would be lucky if she got any sleep at all.

Oh, Father! You answered my prayer, but now what do I do with it—with him? I should be happy, but I'm so confused. I want him back, but I don't know if I could handle it if he went "away" again. Where was he? Do I even want to know? RJ deserves a father he can count on. Can we count on Roger? Will he be there to watch him grow up and do all the things a father should do with his son? What do I do?

Trust.

Trust? Trust Roger? How? I can't.

Jackie rolled over and tried to put both God and Roger out of her thoughts. But what else was there to think about? She got up an hour later and heated a glass of milk and changed for bed; then she crawled between her cold sheets and propped the novel she was reading on her knees. She needed to focus on someone else's life and troubles. It was easy to know what another person should do. Real life was so much harder.

She mentally shook the past and present free and focused on the character's problems.

❧

On the corner of Becket and Glover Streets, Roger watched the glow of the basement light. Jackie was up. He had seen her shadow pass by the window. He longed to go to her, hold her in his arms as he once had, to know his son and be a father to him. He had to believe Jackie and RJ were alive because he had gone away. If he hadn't returned so often to watch them from a distance, they'd still be safe. But his compulsion to see them again and again had endangered them, and now he was between the proverbial rock and hard place with no open door for escape. But some said that when the Lord closed a door He opened a window. And his window of escape was Jackie. He had to wait for the Lord's timing, though. He prayed again for their safety. Now it was more important than ever.

The following morning, he leapt up the front porch steps and rang the bell at nine forty-five. He hoped Jackie wouldn't mind his being early. The first thing he noticed when she opened the door was the dark circles under her eyes; he knew he had caused them. Soon this would all be over, he hoped, and they could live a normal life. If that was possible.

She smiled at him and invited him inside. "I'm glad you came early."

That made his heart dance.

"RJ was up during the night. He's going to need to go down for his nap early."

The dance ended. "Where is he?"

She motioned toward the kitchen. "He's eating a snack before his nap." She led the way. Her loose hair hung to the middle of her back in gentle waves.

He could remember the feel of it between his fingers and longed to touch it again. But he wouldn't push her. She had agreed to let him come over to see his son, and he would respect that whether he wanted to or not. He knew he had to wait. He had raced ahead of the Lord before, doing things his way, and now he was estranged from his wife and son.

RJ climbed out of his high chair and had one foot on the tray. Jackie raced over to him. "RJ! Sit down."

"Out, Mama, out." He held out his arms to her.

She caught him up as the high chair began to tip. His sticky banana-coated hands clutched her around the neck and in her hair. Roger almost laughed. RJ turned and stared at him as Jackie wiped his hands with the dish cloth at the sink. He enjoyed watching her move and interact with his son. A luxury he had missed.

RJ fussed when she set him down to clean the high chair tray.

"Hey, RJ—I'll hold you." Roger reached down and picked up his son for the first time. The boy's eyes widened; then he squirmed and stretched out his hands to his mother. "It's okay. Your mommy will be finished in a minute." It cut him deeply to see his son afraid of him. He had to expect it, but that didn't lessen the pain.

Jackie tossed the dish cloth in the sink. "I'll take him."

Roger reluctantly handed his son to her. He was determined to succeed in his mission; then little by little he would win them over. He had to believe both of these things, or he would give up all together.

"You're welcome to come down." Jackie adjusted RJ on her hip and went downstairs.

When Roger caught up with her at the bottom, he noticed the basement had been redone since he'd left. The couch and dinette set they'd had in their apartment replaced his in-laws' furniture. The flowers he had given her last night sat in the middle of the table.

RJ scrubbed his face into Jackie's shoulder. She rubbed his back. "He's really tired. I should put him down."

"But I just got here. I haven't had a chance to see him."

"I can't help that. He needs a nap."

"May I see him for a few minutes before he has to go?"

She let out an exaggerated breath and sat on the floor with RJ on her lap. "Go get your truck, Honey." He shook his head.

Roger plucked a truck out of a toy basket and sat down with them. "Here's your truck."

RJ turned away from him.

"Does he know who I am?"

"RJ, who's this?" Jackie pointed to Roger. RJ stared at him. "Who is this?"

RJ crawled off her lap and ran down the hall.

Jackie shrugged her shoulders. "I'm sorry. He's usually friendlier than this."

RJ returned with a silver picture frame and handed it to Jackie. "Mama." He pointed to the lady in the long white dress.

It was their wedding picture. Jackie was so beautiful and happy. He wanted to put that smile back on her face. She deserved to be happy. He wished he could return to that day and change the things that had gone wrong. The things he had done wrong.

Jackie pointed to Roger in the picture. "Who's this?"

RJ looked shyly at Roger and back at the picture, then said in a quiet little voice, "Daddy."

His heart skipped a beat when he heard that word come

from his son's mouth. Jackie had taught him who his father was, even in his absence. He didn't deserve either one of them.

Jackie pointed to Roger. "Who is this?" Her voice was sweet and coaxing.

Roger held his breath.

RJ stood so his nose was almost touching Jackie's but didn't turn to look at Roger. "Daddy." His voice was so small and quiet that if there had been any other noise in the room the lone word would have been lost. "Nigh-night, Mama. Go nigh-night."

Jackie gave Roger an apologetic look, then picked up RJ and walked down the hall.

Roger let out his breath slowly. He placed the toy truck carefully back in the basket with the other toys. How could a stupid basket of toys make him feel as if he had a treasure chest filled with gold doubloons before him? Because they were his son's toys. Treasures indeed! *Thank You, Lord.*

Roger scanned the room. Jackie wasn't the pack-rat she once was. He wanted to search the room for what he needed, but he knew it was wrong and not the way God would have him handle this. He had to trust God to work it out. He doubted he'd find what he needed here anyway. The room was almost bare, except for a basket of toys and a few children's books. He picked up their wedding picture and caressed Jackie's outline. "I love you."

Jackie returned and yawned. "We'll have to do this some other time."

He wanted to take her in his arms and ravish her with kisses to thank her for his son. "Tomorrow then."

"Saturday? My parents—"

"The park. Say ten o'clock."

"I don't know."

"I'll wait."

She slumped her shoulders, apparently too tired to fight.

He knew she would be there. Her expression softened as RJ came up beside her. She took him in her arms. "What are you doing up, Honey?"

He draped his arms and head over Jackie's shoulders like a wet rag. She backed up and sat on one end of the couch.

Roger sat down next to her and touched RJ's back. "Is he okay?"

"He's just tired." She readjusted RJ so her arm holding him was resting on the couch. Soon they were both asleep, and Jackie's head bobbed over onto Roger's shoulder.

This was what his life was supposed to be. And he would do everything in his power to have it. He sat for over an hour savoring the life he was meant to have, watching his son sleep.

Then RJ wiggled a little, and his eyes opened slowly and blinked at him. The boy climbed down, and Jackie's head rolled off Roger's shoulder. Then she scooted down until she was curled up on her side. Roger stood.

"Mama seep."

Roger put his finger to his lips. "Shhh. Yes, she is."

"Hungee."

How do you tell a two year old to whisper? "What do you want to eat?" He kept his voice low hoping RJ would get the idea.

"Hot dog!"

Roger winced at RJ's volume, but Jackie remained unmoved.

RJ yanked several times on the small refrigerator until it opened. He pulled out a package of hot dogs and retrieved one, leaving the package on the floor and the refrigerator door open. Then he climbed into the chair with a booster seat and champed off a bite.

Roger put away the package and took the seat adjacent to him. "Do you want a bun to go with that? Some catsup, a little mustard? Chili and fried onions are great on those things."

RJ blinked at him and continued eating, obviously preferring his dog plain. Roger would have to teach him the fine art of eating a hot dog the right way when he was old enough to appreciate it.

After RJ finished his hot dog and Roger gave him a little box of juice, the two sat on the floor by the basket of toys. Roger pulled out the truck, and RJ took it from him. He pulled out a car. The little boy took that. Every toy his father pulled out of the box, RJ took until his lap was full. His father got the idea. They were the boy's treasures, and he wasn't willing to share. Roger would enjoy watching.

"Does your mommy have to go into work tonight?"

"Mama seep."

"Yes, I know," he whispered, hoping it would sink in.

❧

"Yes, Mommy has to work tonight." Jackie stretched out on the couch and rubbed her eyes. It was time for her to wake up anyway.

Roger moved over to the couch. "I'm sorry. I tried to get him to whisper, but I didn't know how."

Jackie sat up. "Two year olds have one volume—loud. They talk loud, they cry loud, and they laugh loud." The laughter was the best.

"I'm sorry he woke you."

It was nice for someone to care about her, but odd just the same. "I need to get ready for work."

"I'll watch RJ. You go ahead."

Jackie went reluctantly, not because she thought RJ wouldn't be okay or Roger would take off with him. She had enjoyed listening to the two of them and had peeked out between squinted eyes at them. A chili dog? That would be a long time in coming. When Roger missed being squirted with the juice box, she almost giggled. She showered and dressed quickly, then worked her hair into a French braid. She wanted to get back out to—her family. She smiled. When she came back out into the living room, Roger sat on the couch reading RJ his favorite book, *Inside Teddy's House.* Tears welled up in her eyes.

She backed up slowly and retrieved her camera. She didn't have any pictures of the two of them. This, she hoped, would be the first of many. She checked the F-stop and put her fingers on the focus ring until they became two sharp images: Roger and a miniature copy. She stared at them through the lens. Father and son. Her mother used to sit with her like that and read; with her father she would stand next to the car as he changed the oil or replaced the water pump, handing him tools. Eventually she helped him even more. What would this pair do together?

Roger's eyes widened in mock surprise as RJ said "ball" and turned the page.

The shutter clicked as she pressed the button. Both heads came up.

RJ scooted off the couch and held his arms up to her. "Mama."

Jackie picked him up as she blinked back moisture. She had broken the spell, but she had captured the moment on film.

Roger stood as well and saluted her. "Nurse Jackie ready for duty." He looked at his watch. "You don't have to leave yet."

"Actually we do. I have errands to run before work."

"I suppose calling in sick isn't an option."

"People are counting on me. I want to see how my patients are doing."

"Jackie the dependable."

She could tell by the way he said it that he admired it in her. She wished he would depend on her and trust her enough to tell her what had happened to him. "Walk us out. I have a surprise."

Roger raised his eyebrows and tried to take RJ into his arms but settled for the diaper bag. "So, is this a good surprise?"

"I'm sure you'll like it."

Jackie opened the door to the garage and stepped into the cool darkness. The light from the house usually lit her way when her hands were full, but Roger flipped the switch, and the room flooded with light. She pulled the side door of her blue van open and dropped her purse onto the floor. "You can put the diaper bag in there too."

"So what's my surprise?"

She smiled. Probably not what he thought, but he would like it. He always had. "It's over here." With RJ still on her hip she walked around Roger to the far back corner. She set RJ down and pulled back an orange plastic tarp from the lump beneath it. "I believe this is yours."

Roger stared at the shiny, black motorcycle. "You kept my Harley?" He touched the tail bar and ran his hand over the leather seat.

"What else would I have done with it?"

He gave her a sideways glance. "You could have sold it."

"It wasn't mine to sell."

"Daddy-cycoe." RJ stepped on the foot peg and tried to climb aboard. Roger hoisted him up and swung on behind him. "Rrrr. I driving. Rrrr."

Roger's expression softened, and his mouth curved up at RJ's usage of Daddy. He didn't realize RJ had no concept of what Daddy meant. It was just a word she had taught him, like any other. Roger would have to teach him the meaning. Good or bad, he would learn that from his father. She could see in her son's eyes that he was confused over the whole daddy thing. Now there was a person to go with it, and he was trying to process this new information.

"I don't imagine it's been run lately."

The gleam in Roger's eyes reminded her of RJ's when he visited a toy store for the first time. It was right to keep the motorcycle, though on several occasions in hurt and frustration she had seriously thought about selling it or swinging a bat at it. So here it sat, like Jackie, waiting for Roger. "Every weekend."

He looked up. His smile broadened. "You've been riding it?"

"Dad has. He's driven it at least once a week. He didn't want the engine or something to dry out." Her father had diligently maintained it in Roger's absence. But she knew it wasn't for Roger that he'd kept it in prime condition. It was for her. His subtle way of helping her preserve her dream of Roger coming back.

"Can I take it out?"

"It's yours. You can do whatever you want with it."

Roger pushed it out into the driveway with RJ still at the handlebars. RJ giggled when it roared to life and rumbled beneath him. Jackie could picture the two of them on identical motorcycles, tearing up the roads. First, RJ would have to be taught to ride a regular bike. Would Roger be around to do that?

Roger shut it down. "It runs smooth. John did more than just drive it."

Yes, he had. He'd babied it in much the same way Roger had.

RJ beamed at Jackie. "I drive daddy-cycoe."

"You certainly did." She plucked him off the seat, then turned to Roger who was still straddling the motorcycle. "We need to go now. You two have fun."

"Wait." Roger put the kickstand down and stepped off. He cupped her face in his hands and kissed her before she could react. "Thank you."

Jackie tottered to her van unsure what to make of it. Her lips tingled. It was calculated, that was for sure. But was she glad he'd kissed her? Or was she angry? She strapped RJ in his car seat and heaved the sliding door shut. Roger was right there when she turned around. She caught her breath.

"I never thought I'd see my Harley again." Roger's eyes were intense and full of appreciation.

So the kiss was a simple thank you, nothing more. Not, *Jackie, I can't live without you.* Or, *Jackie, you are everything to me.*

"I'm going to make things right between us. I promise." He caressed her cheek.

She sucked in a quick breath. It was a promise she hoped he kept. He had always been so confident. She hoped his confidence wasn't misplaced this time.

four

Jackie pulled into a parking space at the hospital and shoved the gearshift into park. The deep-seated ache still gripped her insides. She closed her eyes and pictured Roger standing next to his bike in her parents' driveway sending her off to work. All she could think of, as she watched him in her rearview mirror, was that he was home and she was happy. She had wanted to turn around and never let him out of her sight again. He was back. But could she trust him to stay? Where had he been, and why had he left her? Until he confessed all or proved himself, she had to resist the urge to throw herself into his arms—if she could.

After dropping RJ at the sitter's on her way to work, Jackie had bought blue and yellow balloons and streamers for his birthday. Still tired, she shuffled into the hospital, willing herself awake and alert. The nap had helped, but it was too short. She could use several more hours of sleep. She hoped Dr. Hoon was not on duty, but it was unlikely. It was destined to be a long shift. Maybe she should have called in sick.

As she sat at the nurses' station on the fourth floor thumbing through patient charts, a shadow fell across the blood pressure readings she was reviewing. Roger? She looked up but was disappointed to see Ramona and Dixie leaning over the counter, Cheshire cat grins on both their faces. Why should she assume Roger was around every corner and would show up everywhere her heart wished? He had been back for less than two days, and already she was getting used to his being around or at least the thought of him there. It was all so confusing.

41

"Out with it." Dixie's bobbed blonde hair framed her face in a way that reminded Jackie of a pixie. "Who was the mysterious hunk in black last night?"

Black? Had Roger been in black? He was wearing all black today, and yesterday at the park, he'd had on his black leather jacket. His new color? It suited him, dark, mysterious; it had always looked good on him.

Three more people gathered at the station, waiting. Jackie glared at Dixie. Had she told everyone? When Jackie had returned to work over a year ago, she had moved to a different hospital to avoid having to explain something she didn't understand herself—Roger. If she told them, they would want to know why she hadn't talked about him before and where he'd been and a ton of other questions she couldn't answer.

"Is he some sort of secret admirer?" Ramona cocked her head to one side.

"Well, he's not very good at the secret part because Jackie knows him. And he had flowers for her." Dixie raised her pale eyebrows.

A teen volunteer, a candy-striper, sighed.

How long had Dixie been watching them?

Ramona turned to her. "What kind of flowers were they? Long-stemmed red roses?"

Jackie did not like being at the center of this. "Don't you all have patients to see and other duties?"

They turned to her and hesitated long enough to take a breath. Evidently they realized she wasn't going to be sucked into their conversation and resumed without her.

Dixie answered. "I think they were roses. I couldn't tell the color in the dark, but they looked as if they could have been red."

"He's not a stalker, is he?" Karl asked her directly, a handsome blond orderly studying to be an EMT.

Jackie rolled her eyes. Hardly. Stalkers had to be around, and Roger certainly hadn't been until now.

"Jackie wouldn't go with a stalker. No, he was someone she knows."

Did she ever know him? She flipped the chart closed and stood. "Well, I have patients to look in on." She had already checked on her patients, but seeing them again was better than hanging around the nurses' station while everyone talked about her. She wasn't needed in this conversation anyway.

"We're not letting you go until you 'fess up."

They had blocked her in. She could always jump the counter and leave them stunned. "I really hate to ruin your romantic fantasy. You're enjoying it so much."

"Come on. Tell us." Dixie was like a dog with a bone. Once she got hold of something, it was tough convincing her to let loose.

Now if Dr. Hoon had been around, Dixie would have to let it go. Where was Dr. Hoon when she needed him? Maybe if she suggested that he could be coming down the hall any moment, Dixie and the others would give up. That wouldn't work. They would only corner her later. She could tell them Roger was just a friend, but the roses wouldn't let that one fly. She took a deep breath. "Roger."

"Roger who?" Dixie demanded.

"My husband." She slipped by the astonished group and down the hall. She ducked into the room of the most demanding and irritating patient on the floor. When she came out a few minutes later, Karl was waiting for her.

Karl's broad shoulders were slumped, and he kicked at a speck on the polished linoleum floor. A puppy dog told to go home looked happier than he did right now. "I didn't know you had a husband. I've never heard you talk about him."

To talk about Roger would be to explain Roger, and that was something she couldn't do. It had been too painful to tell people her husband was missing and presumed dead. She held up her left hand to show her wedding ring. "Coming up on four years. We've sort of been—separated."

"And now he wants you back."

That was the impression she had. "He wants to be part of our son's life."

"Then he would have brought a toy not flowers."

The candy-striper approached. "Dr. Hoon wants to see you in his office."

Dr. Hoon disliked candy-stripers. They were pretty decorations that stood in the way of real medicine. That he sent one to summon her was not good. Jackie headed for the doctor's office. He didn't like to be kept waiting. He had been trained in the Marine Corps and didn't realize the staff members were not soldiers. She took a deep breath and knocked on his door. He called her in.

"You wanted to see me."

He sat behind his desk of authority with his hands steepled. "I believe in getting right to the point. You have always been a good nurse. But after last night's performance I wonder if this whole hospital has a decent nurse in it."

She had missed several of Dr. Hoon's requests last night and had to ask him to repeat himself time and again. He had been exasperated by the end of the night.

"I chose this awful shift because you are one of the few competent nurses I can work with."

He picked her shift? He wasn't like poor Karl, was he? She wanted to blurt out, *I'm married!* "I was having a small family crisis yesterday. It won't happen again."

"I would hope not. People are depending on us."

"I know."

"Do you? We have their very lives in our hands. This isn't like flipping burgers. What we do here matters."

"I know." Was that all she could think to say?

"What if we'd had a real emergency?"

Last night had been less than uneventful. But Dr. Hoon didn't want to hear that. "If we had, it would have pushed all other thoughts aside as always. I have no doubt my full attention would have been on the patient. But since there was no emergency, my mind wandered a little." She couldn't help herself. "I will strive harder in the future not to let my personal problems interfere with my concentration here."

The hard lines around his mouth softened a bit. "I'm glad to hear that. Not about the troubles, you understand." He turned his focus back to the file in front of him, dismissing her.

She needed to say more. "My husband was missing, and now he's back."

"I'm glad he's safe." He didn't look up from his papers.

"We're sort of working on getting back together." At least she hoped so.

He looked up over the top rim of his glasses. "I'm not interested in your personal problems as long as they don't interfere with your concentration at work again."

Jackie leaned against the doctor's door after closing it. Stupid, stupid, stupid. Why should she think every man was interested in her now that Roger was back? Who would she suspect next, the seventy-year-old male food server in the cafeteria who wore a hair net? Her shift stretched longer and longer before her.

❧

Jackie parted her hair to start a French braid down the back, one section over the next, and suddenly stopped. Roger had always liked her hair down. Did he still? It was Saturday, and she didn't know if he would show up at the park or not. She let her hair fall and pulled up each side into a barrette. RJ was old enough not to pull her hair, and she didn't have to go into work.

Roger had taken over her dreams last night. He had held

RJ and been every bit the father RJ needed, and he'd held her as well, caressing away her fears and doubts. It was okay he had been away. She understood it all. She had been safe in his arms. But it was only a dream. Dreams did little to fill the empty place that had long since taken up residence in her. They only made her more aware of the void Roger had left. A longing deep inside for more—for things to be the way they were before. Everything was so uncertain now.

She tucked peanut butter crackers, raisins, and two juice boxes in the diaper bag. RJ was upstairs being spoiled by his grandparents, eating pancakes, and watching cartoons with Grandpa. The Saturday morning ritual.

Her mother had on her yellow rubber gloves while she loaded drippy dishes from the sink to the dishwasher. "Did you get the balloons and streamers? If not, I can run to the store today or tomorrow and pick up some."

"I got them yesterday. Blue and yellow."

"Yellow? I thought you were going to get red."

"If you want red, Mother, get red." She didn't care. She was too tired to fight over the trivial.

"You don't have to snap at me. It doesn't matter what color you bought."

Exactly. RJ didn't care, so why should her mother? But she hadn't meant to lash out. Fatigue and the uncertainty of what to expect when she saw Roger, coupled with wanting to get out of the house before her parents grilled her, had caused her to snap at her mother. She knew nothing more than she had the other night, and it would only turn into a big fight. They'd never liked Roger. Had they been relieved to have him out of her life?

A few months ago, her mother had invited a coworker over for dinner, telling Jackie she needed to accept that Roger was never coming back and move on with her life. The poor guy could feel the tension sparking across the table. After he left, she had told her parents she was moving out. Her mother promised not to interfere anymore and asked her to stay for RJ's sake. Now she wished she had stood her ground and had her own place. "I'm taking RJ to the park."

"So early? The fog hasn't even lifted."

"The sun will burn it off soon. I promised him. He'll have all the equipment to himself." She headed for the living room but stopped short at her mother's sharp question.

"You're going to see him, aren't you?"

Jackie swung around to face her. "Him? *Him* is my husband! I need to see where things lead."

"I can tell you exactly where they will lead."

"Mother, this isn't open for discussion."

Her father came in then. "What's the commotion?"

"She's going to meet him."

Her father frowned. "We wanted to talk to you about this." He stood next to her mother. The sides had been drawn. "What actually happened to him? Where has he been?"

"I don't know anything more than I did the other night."

"Are you sure it's wise to go then?" her father said.

"How else am I going to find out if I don't? For two and a half years, I have been walking on eggshells with everyone afraid even to mention Roger."

"Maybe he could come for dinner. We could get everything out in the open then," her father suggested.

Though a diplomatic approach, it may not be best if everything were out in the open all at once, at least not until she knew what everything was. "I don't think that would work right now, Dad."

Her mother jumped on that. "Don't be idealistic. He swooped into your life once before and caught you up, then left you for who knows what. Now he's back without an explanation, and you can just go along with it? Don't be naive."

She gritted her teeth, resolved not to react to her mother in anger. If her mother hadn't protested so much the first time when Roger "swooped" into her life, she might not have jumped into marriage so quickly. She would still have married him, but their engagement would have lasted longer.

She was tired of feeling sorry for herself. What was wrong with wanting to spend a little time with her husband? After all, wasn't his return, with his being alive and well, more important than his absence? "It's time for me to walk with my head up as if life means something to me again." She knew she would have to ask the tough questions and get some answers, but right now she wanted to celebrate.

"So you are going to cast our feelings aside and walk all over us?"

Oh, brother! "I'm not walking on you." Her mother's hormones were erratic these days, and she often took things the wrong way, blowing the simple out of proportion. "I don't want to look back on this when I'm old and wonder what might have been. If that means giving Roger time, then I will." She didn't like to be pushed, and she wouldn't push him—yet.

"So you've thought this through?" her father asked.

"For two and a half years."

Her mother's lips were pursed as if she were in pain, and her arms were folded tightly across her chest. "We obviously can't talk you out of it. You might as well leave RJ here with us while you race toward disaster."

Jackie took a controlled breath. She knew her mother meant well. "Roger is not disaster. You don't know where he's been or what he's been through."

"And neither do you."

She never understood her mother's dislike for Roger. "I'm going now." She walked to the living room archway. "RJ, it's time to go."

RJ jumped up and came to her. "Me go swing."

"Please promise us you'll be careful," her father called to her as she headed for the door.

"John, stop her."

"I can't do that."

"But he's going to hurt our baby again."

"She's a grown woman."

It didn't matter what her mother said about Roger being disaster. She needed to see him again. It would hurt too much if he didn't show. She had been waiting for this for too long. She strapped RJ in the stroller outside. Maybe they'd had a rocky start, but Roger was not a disaster waiting to happen. She had to believe he truly wanted things to work out between them, and he was so good with RJ. Maybe that was all she had. It was enough to start with, she told herself.

The park was empty, the fog thicker here than at the house. The dampness seeped through her clothes. She couldn't see Roger, but then she couldn't see the other side of the park. He could be in the fog out of her sight. That's how she felt the last couple of years, as if Roger were just out of her sight and her reach.

"Swing!" RJ pulled at the safety straps and tried to climb out.

Jackie stopped the stroller and freed him. He ran to the swing and waited for her to catch up. She lifted him in and gave him a push while scanning the fog. Movement in the fog caught her attention. She stared, forcing a shapeless image into focus. The hair on the back of her neck came to life. She resisted the urge to flee. But the harder she stared, the less she could make out.

Then she noticed movement in another section of fog to her left; a shadowy figure formed with a firm stride. Roger! She forgot where she was and had to duck quickly to avoid being knocked over by RJ in the swing. She wasn't a school-girl anymore, but her emotions acted as though she were. He was her husband, she reminded herself, not some adolescent crush. But just the same the feelings were present and strong.

"You were distracted," he said, walking to the swing.

How could she not with that swagger? She felt her cheeks warm.

"You could get hurt that way," he told her.

She took another step back from the swing. "I didn't expect you yet." She wasn't sure he'd even come.

"I've been here since six thirty. I didn't want to miss you." He caressed her cheek with the back of his fingers. "You look happy to see me."

And she thought leaving the house before nine was pushing it, especially when she didn't expect him to be there until ten, if at all.

Roger caressed an invisible hair back away from her temple and cheek. Her skin tingled under his touch. He could still captivate her with his mystical gray eyes. Neither one of them moved, caught in the spell of the fog. What was he thinking? Was he as rattled as he made her feel? Where did they go from here? What was the next step? He hadn't said if he was staying around; she only assumed. What if there wasn't a next step? If his gaze was any indicator, there would not only be a next step but a whole beautiful hike ahead of them. Underneath it all, though, lay the unanswered questions. She pushed them to the back of her mind.

"Higher!" RJ squealed.

Another spell broken.

Roger walked around in front of him and grabbed his feet, holding him suspended. The little boy giggled. Roger pulled him higher and let him go. Jackie pushed from the back. RJ swung back and forth between them. Was this a glimpse of RJ's future, to be shuffled back and forth between his parents? No. She would do whatever it took to give RJ a stable home.

Roger grabbed his son by the feet again. RJ's giggle seemed

to be amplified in the fog. Roger let him loose. "Hey, Kiddo, you want to go for a ride on my motorcycle?"

"Cycoe!" Probably the only thing he would give up the swing for. RJ started climbing out even though he was still swinging. Jackie's heart froze between beats. She grabbed for the swing, but it slipped from her hands.

Roger reached out his arms and latched them around RJ and the swing, catching him safely. "He's quite a daredevil."

"Like his father?"

He gave her a roguish smile. Maybe that was what drew her to him, that aura of danger and mystery.

Roger lifted RJ out of the swing and walked back the way he'd come. Jackie followed with the stroller and the diaper bag. The Harley took shape in the fog. Roger set RJ on it and slipped a child's helmet on him.

"You aren't really taking him for a ride?"

"Sure." He strapped the helmet under RJ's chin and made sure it was snug.

"Can he hold on well enough?" she asked nervously. "I don't think that's a good idea."

"He'll be safe. I won't go fast." He pulled another helmet off the back of the bike and stepped up to her. Jackie shook her head. She knew how intoxicating a ride on the back of his Harley was. She had to resist. He placed it in the seat of the stroller. Then he fitted his own helmet on, swung onto the bike behind RJ, and kicked it to life.

"Roger."

He smiled at her. "We won't be gone long." He checked the street and rolled forward.

A cold hand gripped Jackie's chest as she watched them disappear into the mist. Was this what Roger's return was all about? Had he come back to take RJ? Her parents were right; what did she know about him? The rumble of his Harley faded in the distance. Jackie's heart struggled to beat. *What if*

I never see either one of them again? Lord, bring them back to me.

Minutes later, she swung around at a faint roar from up the street behind her. They came out of the fog just as they had disappeared into it, like a dream coming into focus.

Roger rolled to a stop. "Hop on."

Jackie inclined her head toward the diaper bag and stroller as her heart beat again and she could draw in a breath. "I think one ride is enough."

Roger killed the engine and put down the kickstand. He patted RJ's helmet. "Now don't ride off without me."

"I driving." Her son beamed at her.

Roger took the diaper bag and hung it on her shoulder and looped the helmet strap over her hand. Then he folded the umbrella stroller like an expert. Had he been practicing? He slipped the lower wheels into one of his black leather saddle-bags. She knew it would never stay, hanging out like that. But he strapped it to the tail bar with a bungee cord, then came back for the diaper bag and stuffed it in the saddlebag around the wheels. When he turned back to her, his expression seemed to say, *Come on—you have no excuse now.* He held a hand out to her. "You haven't lost your sense of adventure, have you?"

That she was here at all with him proved she hadn't. The word trust popped into her thoughts. But how? she wondered. How could she trust a man who had hurt her so? Uncertain, she took his hand anyway. Again the allure of danger and the unknown drew her. Jackie climbed on the back, and Roger squeezed in behind RJ.

RJ looked around his father's leather-clad arm. "I drive." Roger's laugh blended with the roar of the bike as he started it. Then they rolled forward into the fog and disappeared, as if they were stepping through a curtain into another world, an unexplored world shrouded in mystery and clouds.

❧

The concern on Jackie's face as he left with RJ had wrenched Roger's insides, and the relief wasn't any better when he returned. But he had to do it—take their son out of her sight and return with him. It was a small step toward her trusting him. He had brought her son back to her.

If RJ hadn't been riding with them, Roger would have driven a little recklessly so that Jackie would hold on to him as she used to. As it was, he could barely sense her hands on his waist, and that was only when they turned corners; otherwise she rested them on her thighs.

It was easy to forget his trouble and believe that what was happening now was his whole life. Indeed this was the life he longed for—and he would trust God and work until he had it and for more than one day. The sun, as if confirming his resolve, cut through the fog and shone down warm on them.

five

Roger drove them to the other side of town to a park with child-sized amusement rides. The rides were ancient but well maintained. After the loop on the train and the airplane ride, RJ wanted to ride the "horsy."

Jackie and RJ clambered onto the carousel platform. Her son picked out a red horse as she knew he would. Roger lifted him onto the seat.

"I driving," RJ said with a big smile.

"Hold on tight," Roger told his son, then stepped off the platform.

"Aren't you coming?" Jackie asked.

"When I was a kid, I ate too much junk before riding one of these. I got pretty sick. My mom tried to warn me." He shrugged his shoulders and grinned. "I haven't liked them ever since. I'll watch from over there."

An old excitement welled up inside her of going round and round, each time anticipating and catching a glimpse of her parents. The old-fashioned music started, and the carousel lurched forward. They were off.

She had one hand around RJ's waist and the other on the pole holding the horse. "Wave to Daddy."

RJ took one hand off the pole, barely waved, and latched back on. Roger waved back.

She turned to keep Roger in her sight. His smile broadened. They were like a regular family on their weekly outing. The only thing missing was a camera in Roger's hand. Why hadn't she thought to bring hers?

As the carousel turned, getting closer to the point where she would briefly lose sight of Roger, something akin to panic welled up in her. That's how it always was in the movies: Someone disappeared, or a menacing face in the crowd would appear then be gone; but the person on the ride knew the danger still lurked out there someplace.

This was ridiculous! Roger would be there. She didn't have to worry. And there he was, right where she had left him. She let out her breath.

"I driving!" RJ shouted to his father as they passed him.

She didn't feel the unexpected and unwelcome fear she had the first time around, but her stomach still tightened when she lost sight of Roger again. Each time they rode around, her stomach knotted, then relaxed when he came into view. She couldn't help it. She tried breathing and talking to RJ. Nothing helped, even though Roger was there every time. She couldn't wait for the ride to be over. The earlier awe and excitement she'd felt when she boarded was gone. She knew at exactly what point the sleeve of Roger's jacket would come into her sight. And there it was. Round and round. How long was this ride going to last?

There—the point where Roger was out of her sight. She swung her head around, and the point where he came back into view was right about—now. She stared. The space he had occupied was empty. She noticed a man with a camera and curly, brown hair a few feet behind where Roger had been, but no Roger. She scanned the people milling about. Where was he? She wanted off. Now!

She looked to the ride operator to catch his eye. She glimpsed him and the man talking to him. Roger! He was chatting with the ride operator.

Finally, the ride began to slow but made another full turn before stopping. She and RJ were on the opposite side from Roger and the operator. Her hands shook as she lifted RJ down. It was stupid to get so worked up over nothing.

Roger met them and took RJ from her arms. "Are you all right? You look a little pale."

"I'm fine. I guess the carousel isn't what it used to be."

He nodded.

After another ride in a little race car on a track shaped like a kidney bean, they set out on the path that circled Little Lake Washington. It was a medium-sized pond that was said to be similar in form to its namesake only on a much smaller scale.

RJ zigzagged across the path ahead of them, looking at rocks and leaves, anything and everything that piqued his interest. Roger cupped his hand around hers. It was a natural action. His warm, strong hand felt so familiar. She tried not to react to his touch either way, as if she hadn't even noticed. But inside, the heat from his hand raced up her arm and spread a warmth through her body.

RJ ran back to her and gave her a rock.

"Ooh, how pretty."

He ran off and brought one back for Roger.

"Thanks."

RJ took off again and stumbled, landing in the dirt. She went to him immediately. He wrangled himself back to his feet and held out his dusty hands to her with tears in his big, gray eyes. Roger's eyes. She gently brushed off each hand.

"Is he okay?" Roger hunkered down beside her.

"He's fine. Not even a scratch." She spoke as much to console RJ as to answer Roger. "All better."

RJ held one dirty hand out to her. "Kiss."

She planted about seven kisses on his tiny palm. "Better?"

He nodded and held out his other hand. She smooched it too. "All better."

"What does a grown-up boy have to do to get that kind of attention?"

Stay with us and never leave. She tried to block out his sultry voice and close proximity, but it wasn't easy when she could feel his breath on her cheek.

She sent RJ back to exploring and continued along the path around the pond.

Roger took her hand again. "You didn't answer my question." There was a playful tone to his words.

She thought it was a rhetorical question. "I don't know. I'll have to think about it. That is if you'll be around." She couldn't help saying it. He needed to remember that everything was not normal. Or maybe she did.

"I'll be around. I promise."

His declaration was surprisingly comforting. But how could it be when he had told her nothing? Was it the Lord granting her comfort? If Roger was going to stick around—and that "if" was a big one in her mind—then perhaps they would have a chance at recovery.

RJ ran back and pulled their hands apart. Squeezing between them, he situated one of his small hands in each of theirs, then tugged on their arms, lifting his feet off the ground and swinging between them.

Roger wasn't expecting it as Jackie had been and was thrown slightly off balance.

After several minutes of swinging RJ, Jackie's arm was tired. "Okay, time to walk on your own," she said. She made sure his feet were on the ground before she let go of his hand.

RJ released Roger's hand and held up his chubby arms to his mother. "Up."

"Mommy's arms need to rest." She rubbed her shoulder.

"Up!" RJ jumped up and down.

Roger grabbed him from behind and hoisted him onto his strong, broad shoulders. RJ screeched as he sailed up to his perch, then smiled.

"How's that?" Roger asked once he had his son settled. RJ giggled.

Jackie thought RJ would want down so she could hold and

comfort him. Instead the boy looked as though he'd always ridden on his father's shoulders. "He's tired and hungry. We should probably be going."

"We can grab a bite here and find a shady spot for him to rest. Unless you have other plans this afternoon."

She gazed into his stormy gray eyes. As soon as she suggested leaving, she knew he would want to stay. She felt some comfort in knowing him well enough to anticipate what he would say. But there was still so much she didn't know—so much he hadn't said—so much she wasn't sure she wanted to know. Was she "better off" not knowing, as Roger had said?

Roger's mouth stretched into a smile, and he wiggled RJ's legs. "You want to get a hot dog, Son?"

"Hot dog!" RJ's voice carried to people near and far.

"Hot dog it is," she said.

&

Roger opened his wallet and paid the hot-dog vendor. Jackie had found a vacant picnic table and was sitting there with RJ. He set the cardboard tray holding the drinks and hot dogs on the table.

RJ snatched his hot dog out of the bun and raised it to his mouth.

"Wait." Roger reached over and put it back in the bun. "Like this." He wrapped both hands around it and pretended to take a bite. "Mmm."

Jackie snickered at him.

He swung his head toward her. "One step at a time. First he learns to eat it in a bun, then add a little catsup, then mustard. Then graduate up to relish and chili and onions. Who knows from there?"

Jackie laughed at him. "Putting his hot dog in a bun is like wrapping it in paper and asking him to eat it."

"You'll see. He'll become a premiere hot dog connoisseur."

"But not today." She looked over sympathetically at RJ.

He turned back to his son. RJ's lower lip was quivering. Roger stripped the hot dog from its bun and handed it back to RJ. "Not today."

Roger made a show of how much he liked his loaded chili dog. RJ imitated him by saying "Mmm" to each bite of his plain dog. And Jackie chuckled at them both.

"Just you wait. I'll teach him to appreciate a real hot dog."

"Maybe you will—when he's older."

" 'Train a child in the way he should go, and when he is old he will not turn from it.' "

"I don't think the Lord had hot dogs in mind."

"It's the principle. Train a child young."

"Why don't you save yourself some grief and wait until he's a teen?"

"But think of all the years he'll miss out."

She cocked her head toward RJ. "He couldn't enjoy that hot dog more if you smothered it in chocolate syrup."

"That sounds disgusting."

She shrugged. "A two year old's two main food groups."

When the hot dogs were gone and the soda consumed and Roger had disposed of the trash, Jackie said, "I need to change his diaper."

He stood up from the table. "I'll get his bag."

"And the stroller."

"I'll be right back." As he walked away from his wife and son, his gut tightened. He turned back. They were still sitting at the table. Jackie smiled and waved, then coaxed RJ to do the same. He waved back and continued to his bike. He couldn't shake the foreboding feeling. He should have listened when Jackie wanted to bring the bag and stroller with them from his bike. He thought they would get in the way, and it would be easy enough to retrieve them if they needed them. He had no idea how much a two year old needed. He had a lot to learn. Leaving his family alone now gave him a deep uneasy feeling. He glanced around. Surely they were safe in a public park. He picked up his pace, retrieved the bag and stroller, and hurried back.

Jackie met him along the way with RJ on her hip. "He didn't want to stay put."

After changing his diaper quickly, she strapped RJ into the stroller. "It won't take long for him to fall asleep once he's forced to stop moving."

"In the stroller?"

"Unless you want to carry around forty pounds of dead weight for an hour?"

She had a point, and in matters of their son she did know best. "The stroller it is." They set out on the path around the lake again. It would take them away from the majority of the activity and noise.

He rested his hand on the small of his wife's back. Jackie didn't seem to mind, although there used to be a time when she would have leaned into him; at least she didn't pull away. It would take time for her to get comfortable with him again and trust him. If she only realized they might have many years together, with God's help, it would be easier on her. He wasn't planning to go anywhere again. Of course he hadn't planned to leave that night; he'd had to go.

"Do you remember the first time we went up to Snow-qualmie Falls?" he asked her.

"It was a Thursday, our third date in three days. We walked on the path at the bottom of the falls. Mist from the thundering water sprayed our faces. Your eyes narrowed ever so slightly. You had a strange, introspective look. I still don't know what it meant. But then it passed. You came back to me with a gentle, satisfied smile and kissed me for the first time."

His mouth stretched in a grin. "I guess you do remember."

"What were you thinking about then?"

"You."

"That's vague."

He hadn't meant to be. Everything that day had come back to her. He couldn't stop thinking about her, even when he wasn't with her. He had never been more aware of another person. "You" seemed to sum up his thoughts because she was part of them all. "You were wearing black jeans and a pink angora sweater. I'd given you my jacket for the ride on my motorcycle. You still had it on. I was trying to figure out the chaos you were causing in my heart. You came into focus, standing in my jacket, the falls crashing behind you, and I knew I always wanted you in my jacket, metaphorically speaking. I hadn't felt a peace like that in years. It seemed natural to kiss you after my revelation. Since the day I met you, almost everything in my life revolved around thoughts of you."

"Is that why you kept pushing for me to keep your coat? I thought you were being so generous."

He laughed. "I didn't feel generous. I felt selfish and hypocritical because I believed I would get it back one day with you in it. The Lord had impressed upon my heart that you were the girl for me. I was disappointed when you wouldn't accept it."

"I regretted it immediately. I always wished I'd kept it."

He shucked off his coat and draped it over her shoulders. "It's yours. It's a little more used and beat up."

Jackie stopped the stroller and touched the collar of his jacket. "I don't want your coat anymore."

"What do you want, Jackie?"

She shrugged. "I don't know."

He saw something flicker in her gaze, but she said nothing more. He suspected she did know but was afraid or unwilling to answer. He supposed it was only fair. He hadn't given her any answers, so why should she give him any?

He gazed at his wife again in his black leather jacket with

water behind her; it wasn't the falls, but the effect was the same. He pressed his lips to hers but didn't linger. He wanted more, so much more, but this would have to do for now.

He was glad she hadn't pushed him for details today—details he couldn't give her. After RJ's nap and a few more turns on the rides and feeling like a real family, it was time to leave. He wanted to get on the highway and head out of town and not look back. Take his family and run. But he needed to trust the Lord to help him finish his mission as well as keep his family safe. So he took them back to the park near Jackie's parents' home.

"Do you have to work tonight?" he asked.

"No, I'm off until Tuesday."

Roger smiled. "Would you consent to dinner? The three of us."

"That would be nice," she said, smiling back.

He had missed her smile. "Six o'clock at Manny's?"

Her smile faded. "Not there."

He sensed her pulling away from him. How could he be so careless? Bad suggestion. "You pick the place."

"I don't know. It's already been a long day."

He took her hand. "Please."

six

Roger stood when he saw Jackie enter the Chinese restaurant they used to visit. Wow! Her dress fit her well, modest yet becoming. He met her halfway between their table and the entrance. "That color looks great on you."

"Thank you. It's mocha."

"What is?" He held out her chair.

"This color is mocha."

"Oh." It looked brown to him. He grinned. He never was good with the vogue names for colors. "Where's RJ?"

"At home with Mom and Dad. He was too tired to come."

So it was just the two of them, and she had dressed up. She had convinced him to meet her at the restaurant to avoid a conflict with her parents. He would face them sooner or later. For now, he needed to know where he stood with his wife. When he finally did face his in-laws, would Jackie stand beside him or against him?

The last time he had sat across from her, he'd presented her with a gift and life was good. In an instant, everything had changed. Now he stared at his menu without reading. He knew what he would order before he arrived. He knew she did as well. They always ordered the same items and rarely opened the menus. But tonight the menu served as something tangible he could hold, as it seemed to do for her.

"I had a good time today," he said after the waiter took their usual orders and their menus.

She nodded. "Me too. RJ's highlight had to be the motor-cycle ride."

"He's really cute, but I can't say I'm disappointed he couldn't come. It gives us a chance to be alone."

She sighed. "How long can we do this, Roger?"

"Do what—exactly?"

"Dance around this gaping hole in our lives?"

Not much longer, he supposed.

Jackie laid her napkin in her lap. "We can go off and do things like today, acting like a real family, but we aren't because we are no longer a couple, and I'm not sure you want us to be. I don't know which way is up anymore. Three days and you have me in a complete tailspin. Where do we go from here?"

He took her hand. "I want to make things right between us."

"But you aren't. I can't move forward blindly. I need answers. None of this makes any sense."

"Ask your questions, and I'll do my best to answer them." He hoped he could fill in some of the hole he had created between them.

"Where have you been all this time?"

He paused until the waiter had served their soup and egg rolls and left their table. "I've been all over."

Jackie slapped her napkin on the table. "I can't do this! Vague answers that tell me nothing—'away,' 'all over.' " She slid her chair out and stood. "Let me know when you're serious."

He stood, too, and grabbed her hand again. "I'm going to tell you more, but you have to understand I can't tell you everything yet." He hoped what he could tell her would be enough.

They sat back down, and he continued. "I've been in Utah, Montana, Oregon, Canada, Chicago, Florida, D.C. I was even in Europe and Australia for awhile and most recently California."

Anger burned in her eyes. He could see she didn't like his answer, but it was the truth. "So, while I was miserable thinking you were dead and almost miscarried RJ because of the stress, you were gallivanting across the country and around the world?"

"It wasn't a pleasure trip, I can assure you. I was working. I took odd jobs wherever I went. I sold books in a little used book shop in Canada; was an orderly in a Chicago hospital; waited tables in Europe, Utah, and Montana; worked at an electronics store in California; delivered pizza in Oregon; and had a variety of other jobs along the way just so I could eat."

"So you weren't delirious or in a coma in some obscure hospital? No amnesia?"

He had to chuckle. "No, nothing so romantic."

"In all your travels you couldn't pick up a phone or send me a postcard: 'Jackie, I've gone off to see the world—be home in a couple of years.' "

"I wrote that first week telling you I had to go away and didn't know when I would return."

Some of the color drained from her face. "You wrote?"

He nodded. Just one was a huge risk. If he had been caught or the letter traced— "Didn't you get it?"

"Oh, I'm sure I got it—along with all the others claiming to be you or some sicko saying they knew where I could find your body and would show me personally but no police. The police said they were all cranks. It's amazing how many sick people there are out there. Your disappearance didn't even make the first section. It was a little blurb tucked between a news item about a nursing home getting new carpet and another one about some rock exhibit at a museum. I'm surprised anyone read it at all."

He, for one, was glad it wasn't front-page news or Jackie would have been in greater danger right from the start. "I'm sorry you had to go through all that. I never imagined you thought I was dead this whole time." There was of course no body, and he had written. But without further word from him, she had evidently thought the worst.

"I got nothing in your handwriting. I would have known."

"I wasn't in real great shape, and my writing was shaky."

"Why? What happened?"

"I was injured." Injured? Half dead was more like it. "Can we leave it at that?"

She leaned forward. "I'm a nurse, Roger—remember? I could've helped."

"Please believe me. I couldn't go to you for help." He picked up his spoon and stirred his soup.

"Is that why there was blood on your cell phone?" Her hand shook slightly as she reached for her glass of water.

"Yes. Can we move on to something else?"

She wrestled her napkin back onto her lap. "I just want a few answers."

He was out of answers he could give her.

The waiter brought their dinner. Neither had touched the food already on the table. He suspected their food would be cold before they ate, if they ate at all.

Jackie set her napkin on the table and stood.

He stood also and touched her arm. "Please don't go."

"I'm just going to the rest room. I promise not to slip out the back door and leave you wondering." She took her purse and walked across the restaurant.

Ouch. He probably deserved that. But he wouldn't endanger her by telling her too much. He would rather have her mad at him than dead. At least mad meant still breathing.

He took a spoonful of soup. It was cold. He pushed it aside and waited for Jackie to return.

ক

Jackie pulled at her bangs. She had cut them too short, and they were just getting back to a good manageable length. She freshened her lipstick. She was stalling. This whole trip to the rest room was a detour. So far she had avoided the most important question, and no vague answer would satisfy her.

She took a deep breath to steel herself and walked back into the restaurant.

Roger held her chair, then sat down again. He handed her the dish of steamed rice.

She wasn't hungry but dished some onto her plate anyway. It gave her something to do.

When they had food on their plates, Roger broke the silence. "I'm sorry I made you worry."

She looked up. "Did you think I wouldn't care you were gone?"

"I hoped you cared, but I had more than just you to think about."

"Thanks a lot." She unwrapped her chopsticks and yanked them apart.

"I prayed for you all the time and assumed you understood from my letter I had to be away."

"Well, now you know I didn't." She pushed the food around on her plate. Though she was fearful of what his answer might be, she needed to know, no matter how painful.

Roger put his hand over hers where it rested on the table. "I'm sorry for everything I put you through. If I could go back and do it all over, I would change many things, starting with our anniversary."

She stared at his hand covering hers. She would change things too. Bile rose in her throat as she prepared to speak. "Was there someone else?" She held her breath.

"What?"

She closed her eyes, then opened them, meeting his gaze. "Did you leave me for another woman?"

He answered quickly. "No."

"While you were gone then, was there someone else?"

His initial surprise softened. "Never. How could you think such a thing?"

"You were gone for more than two and a half years."

"So that automatically makes me unfaithful?"

"Two and a half years is a long time."

He took his hand from hers. "I know it is, but I promise I have been faithful to you."

She wanted to believe him, but with no other answers to fill the void it was hard.

"What about you?" A sudden thin chill hung on the edge of his words.

She looked up into his angry face. "What about me?"

"Have you been faithful to me?"

She flinched at the tone of his voice. How dare he! "Of course I have!" People turned from the tables nearby and looked at them.

"Hospitals are full of single handsome doctors. Doctors disillusioned with their own wives. A young, beautiful nurse, confused and alone—"

"Stop it!"

"Why? It's not so far fetched. One thing can lead to another."

"I have never been with anyone else."

"And neither have I. Why is that so hard to believe? Because I'm a man, and it's in our nature to cheat?"

"If there wasn't another woman, why did you leave and stay away so long?"

"It was business."

A woman she could almost understand. But business? Whatever that meant. She grabbed her purse and stood.

Roger latched onto her wrist. "I could never be with anyone else. You are the only woman for me."

"I don't know where you've been or who you have been with. Since you won't tell me anything, I have to fill in the missing time my own way." She pulled from his grasp and walked out.

She wished he had told her something she could sink her teeth into; then she would know how to feel, instead of this limbo. She yanked open her van door and sat in the driver's seat, not wanting to go home. *Why me, Lord? Why is all this happening to me?*

Roger left the restaurant about five minutes later. She saw him scanning the parking lot. He seemed surprised she was still there. He stood for a minute staring at her. She thought he would come over, but he climbed on his motorcycle and rode away.

Why should she think he would come over to her? To talk? He had apparently chosen not to tell her anything.

❦

Roger slipped in the back of the church. He had followed Jackie and her parents to see which church they would attend, but he hadn't needed to; they attended the same church as always. He sat in the far back closest to the door for a quick exit. Some people here might recognize him, and he didn't want to be greeted. This was how he'd attended church the last two and a half years: come late, leave early, sit in the back. He was rarely noticed except by the pastor and never greeted. He wanted to belong again, not always be an outsider.

He could see the back of Jackie's head where she sat near the front with her parents. He should be up there with her, but now was not the time.

Jackie's accusations and distrust had cut him to the core. He never imagined she would suspect he was unfaithful. Even if he had told her the whole truth, would she believe him? Had too much happened for her to trust him again?

If she can't trust me even a little, Lord, then this is all doomed to failure. Please let her know she can trust me.

He shouldn't have accused her back. This was harder than when he was away. At least then he thought Jackie trusted and loved him. Now he realized the cost of his desire to see justice served. He may have lost Jackie for good.

He watched Jackie rather than listened to the sermon.

During the closing song he slipped out.

❧

Sunday night Jackie caressed RJ's back until his breathing was even. When she was sure he was asleep, she scooted off his bed and went upstairs for the movie. Her parents had rented an old musical. She could smell the popcorn all the way in the basement.

Her father was reaching in the cupboard for bowls to put the popcorn in. "How are you doing, Honey?"

"Fine. Why do you ask?" She took the bowls from him.

"Well, a lot has gone on in your life lately, and I just figured you two had a fight."

She knew he meant between her and Roger, not her and her mother. "Why do you say that?"

"You came home early last night, and you've been moping around all day."

"I have not been moping."

"You've been unusually quiet, and we had to do a lot of talking to get you to come up for a movie." He opened the microwave and pulled out the bag of popcorn.

She sighed. "We didn't exactly fight. I said some things I wish I hadn't, and I'm sure he did too."

"Sounds like a fight to me." He poured even amounts of popcorn in each bowl.

"I just thought he would come by today to talk about it."

"Has he told you his plans?"

"Not really." She picked up two of the bowls in one hand and one in the other.

Her dad retrieved three sodas out of the refrigerator. "What do you want, Honey? Do you want him back?"

"I don't know." She walked into the living room. "I do but on my terms. Not unconditionally."

"That's understandable." He put the sodas on the coffee table.

"I demanded answers and accused him of being with someone else."

"There is nothing wrong with wanting the truth. As his wife you have a right to know. You need to know what it is you have to overcome."

Her life was so confusing. "I don't know what I want. I just wish I could go back and stop him from leaving in the first place." She laid her head on the back of the couch. "Where's Mom?"

"Putting on her nightgown. She likes to be comfortable."

Her mother came out then, and they started the movie.

Jackie sat there watching the movie, but she had no idea what was going on. She kept rehashing the fight, yes, fight, she'd had with Roger the night before. Looking back, maybe she wanted to fight, wanted to make him mad in hopes he would blurt out the truth. She second-guessed everything she'd said and didn't say. Why would he feel he could tell her anything when she didn't believe him and attacked him? He had been hurt, deeply so, at her accusation of infidelity. She didn't understand the hurt in his eyes until he turned her accusation back on her. How deep it cut.

Then he drove away. She had pushed and pushed until he left. Was he gone for good? She had expected to see him today, but there was no sign of him. None. It was as if he had never returned, except she was looking for him now. And he wasn't there.

She stood up from the couch. "I'm going to bed."

Her father pushed the pause button on the remote. "But the movie's not over yet."

"I'll finish it another time." She plodded down the stairs. She was tired, but she wasn't going to bed to sleep. She needed a good cry to mourn her loss—a second time.

≈

Roger stepped out of Chestnut Street Church into the wet

night, needing to get away before the Sunday night service let out. Another church attended unnoticed. This vagabond lifestyle had worn out its welcome. Not that he had ever wanted it. But since being back with Jackie and his son, he wanted nothing more to do with this kind of existence.

Fortunately the rain had let up for awhile. He had parked his Harley a block away under a tree to keep off most of the rain. He hopped on. He had an appointment to keep and drove the two miles to the rendezvous behind an old, closed-up shopping center. He waited.

If Jackie had been spiteful, his Harley would have been the first thing to go. But then she had thought he was probably dead. Still, the fact she kept it meant more than the cycle itself. He had counted everything lost, including his family. *Thank You, Lord. This is the spark of hope I needed. Somewhere deep inside she still loves me, and we will be a family one day.*

"Nice toy."

Roger spun around. "Sweeny." The man had stepped out from the side of the building.

"Do you have it?" Sweeny looked down his long, narrow nose, his curly, brown hair perfectly in place.

"Not yet."

Sweeny's lips twisted into a smug grin. "I have something for you." He reached inside his front pocket and tossed an envelope at him.

He caught the envelope and opened it. His throat tightened. Inside were photographs of Jackie and RJ the first day he approached them at the park. He was in some of them. There were several pictures of yesterday's adventure as well. The series where he was walking away from Jackie and RJ to get the diaper bag nearly undid him. He'd sensed it. Perhaps the Lord had been warning him. He swallowed hard to dislodge the lump in his throat. He reined in his emotions before looking back at Sweeny. "What's this supposed to mean?"

"Nice-looking family. I'd hate to see anything happen to them." Sweeny chuckled. "If I had known about them sooner, I could have been rid of you two and a half years ago."

"I already told you to leave them out of this. I'll get it."

"It's your own fault." His voice held a cold edge of irony.

He knew he should have stayed away for Jackie and RJ's safety, but he had been compelled to come and look. What could it hurt? It had been his downfall, the opening Sweeny needed to find his weakness. And when he was so close to wrapping up his troubles, Sweeny along with them, and coming home for good.

Sweeny squinted his beady eyes. "This isn't nursery school, Villeroy. Your time is running out."

Roger squeezed his hands into hard fists. If Sweeny hurt either one of them, he'd tear him apart with his bare hands. Sweeny already had Moore's blood on his hands. And only the Lord knew how many others. But it wasn't just Sweeny he was after. He wanted the ones at the other end of his leash. This had gone higher than even Moore had realized. His death would not be in vain.

seven

By Monday morning, Jackie scurried around still second-guessing everything she'd said to Roger. No word at all from him on Sunday. She realized she had no way to contact him. Had she pushed him away with her insistent probing the other night at dinner? Was he staying in a hotel or with a friend? Did he even have friends? In their year of marriage she couldn't recall his mentioning any friends. She was so blissfully in love she hadn't noticed anyone, only Mr. Moore, whom she couldn't find when Roger disappeared. But there was Someone who knew where he was.

Lord, please bring him here today. This is the day Roger needs to be here. Today of all days. I know I asked over and over for You to bring him home. I know I seemed unappreciative, but I'm not. Today please do it for RJ.

Jackie went upstairs with RJ and set him in the high chair with a cut-up apple in front of him. She pulled out a chocolate cake mix and prepared it. As she was spooning the batter into the paper-lined cupcake pan, the doorbell rang. She put down the bowl and licked her fingers on the way to the door. Her heart danced at the sight of him, and for a moment, she stared and forgot to breathe. He was here. He was really here. She wouldn't push him again.

"These are for you." He held out a pair of kissing penguins. "I didn't see your collection but assume you still have it."

She took them and pulled their magnetic beaks apart. "They're in my bedroom."

"I'm sorry for the other night."

"Me too." A long moment of awkward silence stretched

between them. "Do you want to come in?"

He followed her into the kitchen.

"Hi," RJ said from the high chair.

Roger ruffled his hair. "Hey, Kiddo. What do you have there?"

He held out a chunk of apple to Roger. "Appoe."

"That looks like a good apple."

"He appoe. He appoe."

Roger looked up at her, helpless. She enjoyed this father-and-son exchange. "He's giving you the apple."

Roger turned back to RJ. "I'm not hungry. You eat it."

"He appoe."

"I'll take the apple." Jackie held out her hand for it.

RJ pulled it back. "No. Daddy appoe."

She looked at Roger, stunned. She thought she could detect more moisture than usual in his gray eyes as he reached out for the gift.

"Thank you."

"You don't have to eat it," she mouthed to him.

"I like apples." He popped it in his mouth.

RJ smiled and went back to gnawing away at his apple pieces.

She smiled at Roger too.

Roger chewed and swallowed the bite of apple; then he held out a store-wrapped package with clowns on it. "When should I give him his birthday present? I'd like to be here when he opens it."

Her eyes widened. "How did you know it's his birthday? I never told you I was pregnant."

"I was at the hospital the day after he was born," he said.

"You were?" She had sensed his presence but chalked it up to wishful dreaming and the euphoria of a new healthy baby, especially after all the difficulties during her pregnancy and the fear of almost losing RJ. "Why didn't you come to see me?"

He shrugged. "It was best."

"Best?" she asked sharply. "Like you were 'away'? Best for whom?"

He sighed.

"Never mind." She let out her breath, hoping she could push the pain away for now. Today was not the day to dwell on it. Roger was here now, and she would be happy with that. "I promised myself I wouldn't do that today." She turned back to the counter and plopped batter into the cupcake pan. This was RJ's day, and she would not spoil it with demands she probably wouldn't get direct answers to anyway.

"I also know that RJ stands for Roger, Jr."

"How do you know the 'J' doesn't stand for his middle name?"

He backed up against the counter, facing her. "Because Cole doesn't start with a 'J.' But what I don't know is why you moved out of our apartment."

She had wanted to stay in the apartment; in case he returned he would know where to find her. "I had complications during my pregnancy. I was on total bed rest for three months and had to quit work. I couldn't live alone and pay the rent."

"I'm sorry I wasn't there for you."

She nodded. Not today. This was supposed to be a happy day, and she didn't want to spoil it with bad memories. But it seemed everything touched on a sore memory; everything was connected. She would focus on the present and deal with the past another time. "Let me get these cupcakes in the oven, and we can go downstairs so RJ can open your gift." She wanted to be in her living room, not her parents'. She finished spooning the batter and slid the pan in the oven. Then she cleaned up RJ, and the trio headed downstairs.

Roger took off his jacket and hung it over the back of one of the table chairs, then sat on the couch with RJ between them.

"Happy birthday, Kiddo." He handed his son the package.

RJ scratched at the wrapping paper to find the edge. Jackie turned the package over and slid a finger under the edge so he could find it. Two seconds later, the gift was free of its wrappings.

"Look! A motorcycle just like daddy's."

Jackie noticed it wasn't child-safe. She was glad RJ wasn't prone to putting toys in his mouth, but she would keep an eye on this one just the same.

The little boy pulled at the packaging but didn't know how to get the shiny motorcycle out.

"You want Mommy to do that?" Jackie reached for the package.

RJ pulled it away from her and held it up to Roger. "Daddy do it."

She knew RJ meant nothing by it, but still it hurt. She had been there for the first two years of his life. Roger had showed up only days ago and bonded instantly with his son through a motorcycle ride. She was glad to see RJ connecting with his father, but she still wanted to know he needed her. Deep in her heart she knew he did. But a daddy-cycoe ride was a powerful thing. She knew all too well.

Oblivious to her ache, Roger cut the tape and untwisted the tie that held the motorcycle to the cardboard back. How could he know she hurt? He was no more a mind reader than she was.

RJ held up the toy. "JJ cycoe." He scooted off the couch. "Rrrr." The Harley raced all over the living room.

Roger turned to her and smiled. "He's quite a boy."

She laughed. "You only say that because he likes motorcycles."

"Not just any motorcycle—that's a Harley." He paused. "Even if he hated motorcycles, I would still think he's the neatest kid around. You know why?"

She shook her head. "Why?"

"Because he is mine." He gazed lovingly at RJ. "That's all he ever has to be for me to love him. All he has to do is exist. He doesn't have to do anything."

Her eyes filled with tears at his wholehearted love. How could she think Roger wasn't ready to be a father? A two-and-a-half-year absence. She wanted to believe he was committed to RJ now. She hoped he was as committed to her. It occurred to her RJ may be the only reason he came back. "If RJ hadn't been born, would you have come back?"

He turned and gazed at her. "Absolutely."

Her chest loosened. She hadn't realized it was tight or that she was holding her breath.

He took her hand. "You are the love of my life." He raised her hand to his lips and placed a gentle kiss on the back of it. A tingle shot up her arm. He caressed her cheek. Her insides fluttered. He had that look he got when he was about to kiss her. But he didn't move toward her. His hand slipped to her shoulder, and he leaned a little closer, tentatively.

Suddenly Jackie jumped. She looked down and saw a diaper in her lap and RJ standing in front of her.

RJ wrinkled his nose. "Icky."

She wrinkled her nose, too. "I can tell." She knew he hated a messy diaper. She stood and turned toward Roger. He had a look of disappointment on his face. "I'll be right back." She followed RJ down the hall to his room.

After Jackie changed his diaper, RJ ran out, squeezing by Roger who had come to stand in the bedroom doorway. She felt her face grow warm. "I should go out there. He might get into something."

Roger stepped aside and followed her back into the living room. RJ was racing his Harley on the coffee table.

The timer sounded from the kitchen, and Jackie hurried upstairs to pull the cupcakes out of the oven and let them cool. When she returned, she picked up RJ's photo album and sat on the couch. "I want to show you this."

Roger sat next to her, and she opened the album cover onto his lap.

The first picture was the hospital photo. RJ's tiny hands were in tight little fists next to his head, his eyes squeezed shut, his skin tinged with a yellow cast. It had taken a month of light therapy and a lot of prayer to clear up his jaundice. She pointed out pictures of RJ lying on the couch, some with her holding him, others of him on the floor, then a few of him propped up in the baby swing. In all of them, RJ's eyes were shut, and he was sleeping. She flipped the page. More sleeping baby pictures. She hadn't realized how many pictures she had taken. She hadn't wanted to miss anything.

Being sick, RJ had slept more than normal for a newborn. He only woke up to eat, and barely for that. He usually fell asleep while nursing and never ate enough.

She flipped another page. Finally a picture with RJ awake. He was looking over her shoulder as she tried to burp him. Her mother had taken the picture. She flipped the page.

"Hold on—not so fast." Roger turned back a page.

"There are more interesting ones, ones where he's actually awake."

"They're all interesting to me." He leaned over to catch a better look at the photos on the page resting on her lap. Then he turned the page.

They looked at more photos of RJ asleep and a few of him awake. In all but one, someone was holding RJ—Grandma, Grandpa, or Jackie.

"Everyone got to hold him."

She could almost hear an "except me" trailing on the end, though he didn't say it aloud.

"I've missed so much."

She knew just the picture to cheer him up. She tried to flip to the back. He put his hand on the pages to stop her. "I want to see them all."

"I wanted to show you one real quick."

He removed his hand. Before she could turn to the back, RJ came over.

He pointed to a picture of himself. "JJ." Then he flipped page after page.

She pulled her hands away and let him. "He's looking for his favorite picture. It's one with—"

Roger held up his hand. "Don't tell me. I want it to be a surprise."

RJ turned one last page and pointed to a photograph at the bottom. "Ball."

Roger laughed. "I should have guessed."

"Now may I show Daddy a picture?"

RJ pointed his little finger at the picture again. "Ball."

"Yes, it's your ball." He would keep talking about that picture if she didn't distract him. "Now go get your ball. It's in your room."

RJ ran down the hall.

She leafed through several more pages close to the end. The book was nearly full. She would have to start another one. She pointed to the last photo that had been slipped into one of the sleeves.

Roger drew in his breath at the photograph of RJ and him seated on the couch reading *Inside Teddy's House*. "You had it developed already."

"The magic of one-hour photo. I was at the end of the roll." She had shot the last few frames, anxious to see how this one turned out.

RJ plopped his ball in the middle of the album. "Ball."

Roger clambered down on the floor and played ball and gave him "horsy" rides until lunch.

She served RJ his usual plain hot dog and some strawberry

yogurt. Roger made no comments about the topping-less hot dog. She pulled out some luncheon meat and started to make sandwiches. "Are you hungry?"

Roger looked up at her with a smile. "Starved."

It felt strange to sit there as a family eating a meal together. It was something she looked forward to getting used to.

After lunch, Roger finished thumbing through the photo album. RJ watched a video for a few minutes until time for his nap.

Jackie always sang to RJ when she put him to bed. She felt self-conscious doing so now with Roger standing close by. But her son needed his routine. It had been disrupted enough lately. She tried to take his new toy from him, but he clung tightly to it. She made him promise not to put it in his mouth and go right to sleep. She was thankful that soon after his first birthday he'd stopped putting toys and other objects in his mouth. RJ tucked the motorcycle in the crook of his arm like a teddy bear. Evidently there was a Harley gene in the Villeroy line.

As they walked down the hall, Roger whispered near her ear, "Why didn't you ever sing me to sleep?"

She smiled. "Because you're not two years old. But if you're nice, I'll let you lick the frosting knife."

"Is it chocolate?"

"Of course."

Roger accompanied her upstairs. As she iced the cupcakes with a thick layer of frosting, he fiddled with the kitchen towel that hung from the oven handle, making sure it was centered and even. They didn't seem to have much to talk about with RJ napping and Roger tightlipped. She would save that discussion for another day. Stay in the present. "So what have you been doing since you came back? Are you working?" It seemed like a simple, innocent question, but she asked it like some prying ninny. What else could she ask and not seem like she was pressing him?

"I'm working. You know me—I can't sit idle."

Do I? "Are you working for Mr. Moore again?" *Doing whatever it was you did.*

He hesitated, and a shadow crossed his face. He pulled the towel from the oven handle and wrapped it around his hand. "I never stopped."

Never stopped! So Mr. Moore took Roger away from me and sent him all over the world. Another day, she reminded herself, not RJ's birthday.

She wanted to shake off the clouds and have fun today—and pull Roger out of his sudden melancholy. She scooped more frosting from the white plastic tub, but instead of picking up a cupcake she touched the knife to Roger's nose.

He stopped playing with the towel and raised his gray gaze slowly to her. "Why did you do that?"

She turned around, pretending to be deeply involved in icing the next cupcake. "You still like chocolate frosting, don't you?"

He wiped his nose and licked his finger. "Yes, but not on the end of my nose."

"I recall making a cake for you, and someone ate half the frosting, and I didn't have enough to finish."

"Your cakes are good enough to stand on their own without frosting."

"Betty Crocker's and mine."

He held his hand down, and she stood mesmerized as he twirled the towel into a twisted length. "What are you doing?"

"Me?" He arched his eyebrows, widening his steel gray eyes. "Nothing."

That innocent act wasn't going to work. "Don't even think about it." She never could best him in a towel fight. "I don't even have a towel."

"You started it."

She backed out of the kitchen and into the dining room. He followed her around the table and into the kitchen again, twirling the towel tighter and tighter. Finally he had her in the corner by the refrigerator. "Are you going to say you're sorry for frosting my nose?"

She giggled. "But I'm not!" This was the playful man she had married. How could she apologize for that? Without a towel she had only one offensive move with which to protect herself from his accurate snap. She charged him. Without distance between them he had no weapon. She pushed him back against the counter and snatched the towel from his grasp. She stepped back to twirl the towel, but his arms latched tight around her waist.

"Oops." She looked up slowly into his stormy gaze, and her breath caught.

"What are you going to do now?" he asked.

Nothing. Just stand and stare. Let him make the next move. And move he did, ever so slowly toward her lips. Too slow. Her stomach tightened. She could feel his warm breath caressing her face. Her heart threatened to smash through her chest. She could wait no longer and reached up to meet his lips. She still didn't know why he left or where he had been, but one thing she sensed on some unconscious level—he had come back for her, and that was what mattered. She slipped her arms around his neck, and he deepened the kiss. It was a hungry embrace, two and a half years overdue.

The door from the garage slammed, and they jumped apart like a pair of teens. "Mom!"

Holding a grocery bag in her hands, her mother glared at Roger.

Roger stepped forward. "Josephine, let me help you."

"Don't you dare. And don't try to sweet talk me as you apparently have my daughter."

"Mom, please—"

"This is my house, and he's not welcome here. I come home early to help get things ready for my grandson's birthday to find the two of you clutched together. He's caused enough trouble. I would think you of all people would be keenly aware of that fact." Her mother turned on Roger. "Get out before I call the police."

Jackie opened her mouth to protest.

"It's okay. I'll go." On his way out he turned back to her. "I won't go far. And I will be back."

After he left, Jackie turned to her mother. "I can't believe you did that!"

Her mother set the bag on the counter. "Someone has to let him know he can't waltz in and out of your life without consequence. You deserve to be treated better. He'll think twice before hurting you again."

And maybe think twice about wanting to come back. "You know what, Mom?" An idea formed as she spoke. "Tomorrow I'm going apartment hunting." She should have stuck to her guns and found an apartment two months ago after that blind-date fiasco.

Her mother pulled out a bag of cheesy puffs, RJ's favorite. "Be reasonable."

"I'm tired of being reasonable and practical and sensible. I want my husband back, and he wants me."

"Want him back?"

"He is my husband, and I love him. I always have. I've just realized how right this is." For better or for worse she had vowed. "I belong with my husband. For good or bad I'm supposed to be with him. It's weird, but I know everything will be all right now." *Whatever took him away, he came back for me.*

Her mother continued to pull items from the grocery bag and put them away. "So you would throw caution to the wind. You did that three and a half years ago, and it came back and bit you—hard. And it will again. He left you once; he'll leave you again. You have RJ to think of this time. He needs a stable home."

"RJ needs to know his daddy loves him. How can he if his grandma is always berating his father?"

"He's pulling you in the way he did before, except this time he's using RJ."

"He's not using RJ. Why do you always think the worst of him?"

"He has never shown anything but the worst." Her mother pulled two large cans of spaghetti-Os with meatballs out of the bottom of the bag—RJ's favorite meal. They all were served their favorite dinner on their birthday. Except Roger. Her mother had never bothered to ask him what he liked.

Jackie shook her head and headed for her refuge. "I hope to find something by the end of the week and move my stuff this weekend."

"You're making a big mistake racing back into this so fast."

"Mine to make."

"I don't want to say I told you so, but—"

Jackie spun around. "Then don't!"

Her mother pursed her lips. "I can't say anything to you without your flying off the handle and doing something rash. Just remember your father and I were here for you when you needed us. If you do this, I doubt we'll be willing to pick up the pieces again when you're so callous with our feelings."

In her mother's eyes, Roger would never be good enough for her. She dismissed her mother's words with a wave of her hand and hurried downstairs.

eight

Roger threw away his trash and stepped outside the sandwich shop.

Sweeny sat atop the Harley. "Nice piece of machinery. I've always wanted one of these."

Well, Sweeny wasn't getting his. "Get off."

Sweeny chuckled and removed himself. "I want the disc."

"I don't have it yet."

Sweeny made a clicking noise with his tongue. "I know your family means more to you than that. It would be a shame if they had an accident."

"Leave them out of this." He clenched his teeth together so hard his jaw hurt.

"A son should have a father. Too bad you won't be around to raise yours. But your wife's pretty. She'll find someone to raise him."

His anger boiled. He would raise his son. "I'll have it for you in twenty-four hours."

Sweeny looked at his watch. "Three o'clock tomorrow afternoon. If I don't have what I want, don't expect to find your dear Jackie and RJ where you left them."

"If you touch either one of them—"

Sweeny raised his eyebrows. "Clearly you're in no position to make demands. I hope you haven't spilled your guts to that pretty wife of yours."

"She doesn't know anything."

"She'd better not. If I get wind she even suspects anything, her life won't be worth any more than yours."

"Stay away from her. I've told her nothing."

"The clock is ticking, Villeroy. Don't disappoint me."

He could guarantee Sweeny would be disappointed. He hadn't spent nearly four years on this operation to let the likes of Sweeny pull it out from under him. No, Sweeny was never good enough to best him. And Sweeny's biggest mistake came when he threatened his family. He would finish this job and see Sweeny and all the others behind bars. Then he would make amends with Jackie and work on getting his life back.

&

Roger drove up Glover Street and stopped in front of the Johnson household. Facing his in-laws was more nerve-racking than confronting Sweeny. The door opened, and Jackie stepped out, motioning to him that she'd be there in a moment. Then she disappeared inside the house. He could wait here on the street, and she would come to him. *Thank You, Lord. I hope the rest of the evening goes as smoothly.*

The door opened again, and Jackie's father came out and down the walk. Maybe it wasn't going to be so easy. He turned off the motorcycle and dismounted. "John."

"Roger." His father-in-law's smile failed to reach his eyes. He had developed a bit of a paunch on his slight frame. "She's getting a jacket."

"Thanks for taking care of my bike. It runs great."

"It's a nice piece of machinery." An uncomfortable silence stretched between them. "You let things sit too long, and they aren't the same as when you left them."

Jackie wasn't a thing, but he got the point. "No, but with a little TLC they can be as good as new."

"Some take more work than others, hard work, and a person could give up too soon." The older man raised an eyebrow.

"But the effort is worth it."

"If a person gave up, things could be worse than before."

"I'm not a man who gives up easily." If at all. He would

spend the rest of his life proving it to Jackie. If the Lord gave him that chance.

"Good."

Jackie came out and joined them. She wore her matching black leather jacket he had bought her after they were married.

Her father looked at her, then back at Roger. "We'd like to invite you to dinner."

"Josephine's not too keen on me," Roger said.

"She's had a chance to cool off."

He nodded. "Then I look forward to it."

"Jackie's next night off is Saturday. How about then?" his father-in-law asked.

"Sounds good." It would give him enough time to finish what he needed to do and let things start settling down.

Jackie hopped on behind him, and they drove away. She wrapped her arms around his waist and rested her head against his back the way she used to. He wanted to keep driving. He stopped some twenty miles away at a remote pond tucked in the pine trees they used to frequent. He stood for a long time gazing at the moon's reflection on the pond with Jackie snuggled up to his side. He didn't want to spoil it yet with talk.

❧

Things had gone well this morning—until her mother returned home. She was glad Roger had come back again today and not waited until tomorrow. She could tell he was being introspective. Though she didn't know his thoughts, she sensed they were heavy.

Roger shifted his position slightly and cleared his throat. "We need to talk."

This was it, the defining moment of their future. The tone of his voice told her so. And intuition told her she didn't want to hear it. No—she wanted to but not yet. She turned toward him.

"It doesn't matter right now." She placed both hands on

either side of his face, and he put his around her waist. She just needed to touch him and be touched. She needed the connection. She drew closer and kissed him.

Roger pulled her closer still and deepened the kiss. She didn't want to let go, but he pulled back from her. "Jackie, it does matter."

Not yet. She tried to step away from him, but he held his hands fast.

"I'm in a bit of a fix. You know that so-called rock and hard place?"

She cocked her head to the left. "What's that supposed to mean? A fix? Like trouble? Like a bloody cell phone? Like 'away,' 'all over,' and 'it was best?' " Instinct told her to run. She stepped away from him this time. This was why he came back! Because he was in a fix! She took another step back. No! He came back for her and RJ—because he loved her. He had to. Another step.

"I need your help." He took a step toward her.

She stepped back again, shaking her head. No, he came back for her, just for her. The pine needles crunched beneath her shoes as she continued her retreat.

"Just one small thing. That's all I need." He held his hands out in appeal as he approached.

One small thing but not her. She turned to flee.

He caught her quickly. "I'm sorry it has to be this way."

Tears burned her eyes as his touch burned her heart.

"There was an envelope, Jackie, in my dresser drawer. I need it!"

Tears came free and cascaded down her cheeks. He hadn't come for her after all. She let the well-worn veil of numbness fall over her.

"The envelope, Jackie—what did you do with it?"

Envelope?

"Please, Jackie, remember."

There was no envelope. Only her. "It got thrown away. A lot of things did when Mom and Dad helped me move."

Roger's hands slipped from her. "No." His single utterance held only despair.

She wanted to say she was sorry, but she wasn't. With an ache she had never known before, she turned and walked away, through the darkened woods away from this stranger she had thought she loved. Anger boiled inside her. How could he do this to her?

He caught up to her. "Are you sure you threw it away? You save everything."

"I can't help you, Roger. You can go away again. Sorry you wasted a trip." She slapped at the tears coursing down her face.

Roger cupped her elbow. "I'll take you home. I've got some fast figuring to do."

She yanked free and kept her feet pointed toward home. Her parents were right in cautioning her against rushing into marriage with a man she hardly knew.

"You can't walk all the way."

She gritted her teeth and balled her fists. "Watch me."

"It's over twenty miles." He stopped.

Before long she heard his Harley roar to life, then pull up beside her. "Get on. I can't let you walk."

She stopped and faced him. "Sure you can. Just ride off into the sunset or sunrise or whatever direction you came from, and don't worry about me."

He cut the engine. "I'm taking you home." He held out her helmet to her.

She held up her hands in refusal and resumed her trek. "Don't worry yourself about me."

He caught up and walked beside her. "I understand you're upset with me, but don't you think you're overreacting a little here?"

She stopped short and planted her hands on her hips. Overreacting would be to scream and yell as she felt like doing. "I don't have it."

"It's just an envelope."

"Just an envelope! Then why do you want it so bad? I'll buy you a box of envelopes. If it weren't for that envelope, would you be standing here with me?"

He opened his mouth but said nothing.

"I didn't think so."

"You don't understand."

"Exactly! Because you have chosen to tell me nothing. I've been away! What am I supposed to do with that? You leave me and come back for an envelope, and I'm supposed to be happy?"

"It's not like that at all."

"Just leave us alone. RJ doesn't need a daddy who may or may not be around." He probably wouldn't be now that she didn't have a stupid envelope. She wished he had never come back.

&

Jackie pulled open Roger's sock drawer. Digging to the bottom in the back, she slipped out a folded white envelope. So this was what brought him back. She unfolded it and dumped out the three-inch mini CD-ROM disc into her hand. She sat at Roger's computer and put the CD in the disc drive. Maybe she would have better luck than she had two and a half years ago. She stared at the box demanding a password. She tried Roger Cole Villeroy. She used her name, her birthday, their anniversary, the date they met, the date he left, Moore. She even tried her parents' names, birthdays, and anniversary.

She sat back and stared at the cursor blinking at her, taunting her. She drummed her fingers on the mouse pad. She had racked her brain two and a half years ago without success. *Lord, help me figure this out.* What else or who else had ever been important to him? Family. But he didn't have any. No siblings, and his parents had died years ago along with his first fiancée.

Roger had told her that after the girl died with his parents he hadn't found much to live for until he met Jackie. He didn't want to waste time with a long engagement. He'd regretted it the last time.

Swallowing hard, Jackie leaned forward and typed in the anniversary of her death. She took a slow even breath before hitting enter. Access denied.

What should she do now? She had a mind to snap the CD in half and give it to him that way. Or she could always hold it hostage to keep him around.

She typed in significant historical events and dates. This hit-and-miss approach was not going to work. She needed a system. She typed in January first and the year Roger was born. She changed only the year until she reached the present and started over with January second. She would find the password if it took her all night.

It was two A.M., and Jackie started back to consciousness, realizing it had been nearly an hour since she had last made a key stroke or an attempt at the password. She rolled her shoulders and tipped her head to one side, then the other. Her neck made several consecutive cracks. She walked across her bedroom and stared at the computer from a distance—Roger's computer. She shook her head. She knew she would never figure it out, but she knew someone who might.

Sitting back in the chair, she pressed a button, and the CD-ROM drawer opened with a whir of the motor. She dropped the mini CD-ROM disc back in the envelope and scanned her bedroom. Where to hide it until she could take it to her computer-expert acquaintance?

nine

It was dawn when Roger unlocked the last motel room. In one night he had rented rooms at seven different motels. He hoped that was enough. He carried in the bag of food and supplies he'd bought and set it in the corner, as he had in each of the other rooms. The room looked like all the others. It was an end unit with a window in the bathroom big enough to crawl through.

He was beat and wouldn't call Sweeny for another two hours. He set the alarm on his watch and stretched out on the bed. His sleep was intermittent but would have to do. The alarm sounded. He picked up the motel room phone and dialed Sweeny's cell phone number. "I've got the disc."

"You're early. I expected you to wait until the last minute."

He could detect a smile in Sweeny's voice. "Why wait when I have it? I want this over as much as you do."

"Meet me at—"

"I'll pick the place." Roger gave him an intersection and told him to meet him on the southeast corner. "If you want this, be there at nine-thirty."

"I can't get there from here by then."

"I think you can. Better hustle." He hung up but not before he heard Sweeny curse.

He locked the room behind him and pocketed the key.

He had to stay sharp today, and sleep obviously wasn't the way that would happen. Everything had to go precisely right for the timing of his plan to work. *Lord, I put these plans in Your hands. Help me succeed in keeping Jackie and RJ safe today.*

It was nine-thirty, and by now Sweeny would be waiting impatiently at the rendezvous. Roger turned onto the street and parked down from where the man was standing on the corner. People bustled by the figure in the gray-tailored suit unaware of the evil that lurked there. He may try to fool everyone else in that getup, but Roger knew him. He studied the man while staying out of his sight. He almost hoped it would start raining. That would really irk Sweeny. But the clouds weren't ready to give up their precious water. Sweeny would wait a little longer before he went after Jackie and RJ.

Roger looked at his watch. Timing had to be perfect. Just a minute or so longer. Sweeny looked at his watch and balled up his fists. Roger engaged the clutch and moved with traffic until he reached the corner.

Sweeny scowled and stepped over to the curb. "I don't like to be kept waiting."

He shrugged. "Traffic."

The man clenched his jaw. "Where's the disc?"

He reached into his jacket, then stopped. "You'll leave my family out of this?"

"Have you told her anything?"

He shook his head. "Nothing."

"Then they should live long lives." Sweeny wiggled his finger for Roger to fork it over.

He pulled his hand out slowly.

Sweeny snatched the disc. "Without you, of course." He raised his right hand hidden inside his coat pocket.

"I wouldn't do that if I were you," Roger said. "Your keepers couldn't have been too happy that you killed Moore without getting the disc."

Sweeny's lips curled up into a smug grin. "But I have the disc this time. I can pull the trigger and be gone before anyone knows who's been shot, let alone who shot you." He chuckled nastily.

"But the disc is useless."

"What!" Sweeny pushed his gun so hard in his pocket, Roger thought it might break through. "You double-crossing—"

Roger had held back a trump card. "Without the password you won't be able to verify the data. Your employers won't be happy if they don't know what they have."

Sweeny's lips thinned, and his nostrils flared. "If you think withholding the password is going to keep you alive—"

"It will give me a head start. The pay phone across the street will ring in thirty minutes. If you want the password, I recommend answering it."

"I don't like games, Villeroy." Sweeny's face turned red with fury.

"You'll have to play this one to get what you want and save your neck."

Sweeny's eyes blazed amber fire. "There's no place in the world where I can't find you. I did before, and I will again."

"Thirty minutes." He engaged the clutch and rolled forward.

"I'll find you, Villeroy—anywhere."

Roger half expected to feel the blow of one of Sweeny's bullets in his back. But the man needed him alive for now. He just hoped Sweeny realized it.

BANG!

Instinctively Roger ducked and looked in the direction of the shot. Black smoke was drifting up from the tailpipe of an old green Chevy. He could imagine Sweeny laughing at him for being so jumpy, if he was still watching. Roger didn't care. He had to make the best use of his time. He hoped Sweeny would wait for the call.

After twenty-five minutes, Roger was in place. He stood at a pay phone a few blocks from Jackie's house. He waited two more minutes, then dialed the other pay phone. He couldn't press his luck with Sweeny any more than he already had. The man might go after Jackie and RJ out of spite.

He picked up on the first ring. "This better be you, Villeroy."

"Moron." Roger hung up and climbed back into the borrowed pickup. Let him figure out if he was calling him a name or giving him the password. He had picked the password with Sweeny in mind.

Roger parked the truck up the street from Jackie's and wrestled a bouquet of balloons out of the cab. The balloons would hide his approach. He could get Jackie to let him inside once she had opened the door. As he ascended the steps, he saw his mother-in-law through the window walking from one room to the next. What was she still doing home? He tried to duck and hide, but how could he with all these floating balloons? He did an about-face and retraced his steps, hoping his mother-in-law wouldn't look out the window. He opened the passenger door and stuffed the balloons back inside.

Did Josephine have the day off? His plan did not include her. He looked at his watch. How much time could he afford? Not much. The only reason Sweeny wasn't already here was because he couldn't get here and back in time for Roger's phone call. So how was he supposed to deal with his mother-in-law? He jumped back into the truck and repositioned it with the garage in view. He looked at his watch again and rubbed his face with both hands. She would leave. She had to.

After twenty minutes, he knew he couldn't wait any longer and reached for the door handle. As he did, the garage door rose, and Josephine Johnson backed out. Roger had already wasted too much time waiting for her to leave. He slid down in the seat of the truck until she drove by, then slipped out and walked around the corner to the front of the house with the balloons. He rang the doorbell and held the balloons in front of his face. He rang the bell again. "Come on, Jackie— answer the door. I know you're still home." He scanned the street for any parked cars nearby that looked out of place.

The door clicked open, and he heard her sigh. Jackie took the bouquet, but when she saw who was behind them her smile faded. "I'm not up for this today."

He stuck his foot in the way as she tried to shut the door. "Jackie, please. It's important." He didn't have to push much for her to relent.

She walked away from the door.

He followed her in and down to the basement. "Where's RJ?"

"Playing in his room." She folded her arms across her chest.

He didn't have time to coax her. They had to get out and fast. The bogus CD he had given Sweeny wouldn't fool him long. But maybe in Sweeny's eagerness to show off his victory prize, Roger had more time than he'd figured. He hoped so. "Get RJ and his diaper bag. And get your leather jacket." It was laying there on the arm of the couch.

She pulled her brows together. "Why?"

"I'll tell you once we're on the road."

She stuck out her chin defiantly. "We're not going with you today. I have to be at work in a few hours."

He could tell this was going to be a battle of wills. A battle he couldn't afford to lose. "You won't be making it into work tonight."

"What? I can't just not go in."

He raked his hands through his hair. "There isn't time to argue. Where's the diaper bag?" He scanned the room and spotted it near the stairs. He slung it over his shoulder and turned back to her. The color had drained from her face. Her gaze was locked on his side—the side that held his gun under his leather jacket. He had hoped to spare her this ugliness. "Let's go."

She stumbled backward. "Wh–what if I refuse?"

Was she testing him to see if he would wave his Glock at her? What kind of a monster did she think he was? "You have no choice—like me."

She sat down on the couch. "I'm not going."

Her bravado wasn't fooling him. And he wasn't going to stand there and argue with her. She would go in the end. He walked down the hall and into his son's room. RJ sat on the floor with several vehicles lined up in front of him.

"Hey, Kiddo. You want to go for a ride on my motorcycle?"

RJ jumped up. "Daddy-cycoe."

"Get your coat."

RJ pulled his little coat off the back of the doorknob while Roger opened the top dresser drawer. He grabbed several pairs of tiny socks and stuffed them in the diaper bag, noting the bag was full of diapers. Good. He packed a couple of extra shirts and bib overalls. What else could a two year old need? He turned back to his son and scooped him up, the Harley securely in his tiny grasp.

"What are you doing?" Jackie demanded, standing in the doorway. "Put him back! I won't let you take him away from me!"

"I'm taking both of you away. Get some shoes and come on." He walked from RJ's room back to the living room.

"Why? I know my parents aren't eager for you to be back without some answers, but they wouldn't stand in the way of our getting back together."

"This has nothing to do with your parents or getting back together. It's about keeping you and RJ safe."

"We're safe here."

"No, you're not. Where are your keys?" She had no idea how much danger waited out there for her.

Jackie only stared at him. She reached over and picked up the phone. "I'm calling the police."

He put his finger on the button. "Don't make this difficult. You'll only scare RJ."

"You're the one who'll scare him."

"Your keys." He held out his hand.

She grabbed her purse, clutching the keys in her hand. "Please don't do this."

He snatched the keys from her grasp. "I wish I didn't have to. Now come on." He headed up the stairs.

"You don't have to."

The panic in her voice cut him to the core. He walked into the garage, opened the van, and set RJ in his car seat. "Buckle him up and strap in next to him." She was carrying a pair of white tennis shoes with her purse. He slid the door shut and stepped in. He took a deep breath before pressing the button on the garage-door opener, then backed out onto Becket Street. After he passed Glover Street, a grayish sedan pulled in behind him. Sweeny, no doubt. As much as he wanted to gun it, he kept to the speed limit. This was not the vehicle to try to outrun him in. Sweeny mustn't suspect he knew he was back there. And he would know soon enough if it was indeed he.

"Jackie, I'm not who you think I am." He kept one eye on the gray sedan.

"A raving lunatic?"

"An electronics consultant."

"I may be slow, but I figured that one out," she muttered under her breath. He still heard; she probably wanted him to.

"I've been working on a case—"

"Oh? Like the CIA or something?" she asked sharply. "You expect me to believe that?"

He took a slow breath at her remark. "No. Like a PI."

"So now you're telling me you're a private investigator?"

"Was. I quit." The gray sedan disappeared in the traffic. Maybe it wasn't Sweeny after all.

"It doesn't sound to me as if you quit," she snapped.

He took another deep breath. He was not going to snap back at her. "A buddy of mine from college asked for help. I was restless and decided it would give me a chance to figure out what I wanted to do with my life."

"And have you?"

Where had that sedan gone? "Have I what?"

"Figured out what you want to do when you grow up?"

He couldn't blame her for not believing him. It would take awhile for her to digest all this. "I still want to work with kids. Maybe teaching."

"That's a nice I'm-ready-to-settle-down kind of answer. Just the thing a wife likes to hear," she said in a mocking tone.

He looked again for the gray sedan. "Sarcasm doesn't become you."

"Nor fairytales you."

If he didn't know Sweeny so well by now, he would dismiss the gray car as coincidence and breathe easier. But the man was relentless. He would not stop until he had silenced Roger permanently. It was better to err on the side of extreme caution. "The point is, I'm sorry for getting you mixed up in all this."

"Mixed up in what, Roger? A kidnapping? I'm the kidnappee not the kidnapper." Her words were clipped and stiff.

"I'm not kidnapping you. I'm trying to keep you safe."

"From whom? The bogeyman?"

He could describe Sweeny as that.

"If you aren't kidnapping us, then stop the van and get out."

"I can't do that."

"You mean you won't." Her voice rose an octave.

This was getting them nowhere. "I'm trying to take responsibility for my actions. I never should have married while working on this case."

An eerie silence blanketed the back seat. Jackie stared out the window with her arms folded tightly across her chest. The silent treatment. RJ didn't seem to notice the tension between his parents and continued to play with his motorcycle.

"What I mean is I should have waited until—"

"I know exactly what you mean. It would have been better if you'd never come back. At least then I could still imagine you were once in love with me."

"I do love you. I always have." Things were worse than ever between them, but at least she was safe whether she liked it or not.

"Right. You should've dropped me a postcard saying you'd died someplace."

"Jackie."

"Don't!" she barked "I don't want to hear any more. I can't tell truth from your fiction."

"It's all truth."

She grunted, and he thought it was best to let it go for the time being. He didn't want to make it any worse.

The sedan reappeared just before they pulled up to the car wash. It had to be Sweeny. How had he managed to follow for so long without being seen? Roger just hoped his plan worked and punched in the car-wash code he'd obtained earlier.

Jackie sat silent—mad or frightened, he couldn't tell. The roller brushes spun to life and started beating the van.

"I thought you didn't like this kind of car wash because it scratches the paint."

She sounded more angry. That was good. He didn't want her scared. "I don't, and it does." It had taken some searching to find this one. "Unbuckle RJ."

She scrutinized him but obeyed. "Why?"

"We're going to be getting out." The brushes rolled overhead.

RJ was unbuckled, and she was working her seat belt free. "In the car wash!"

"Just hurry up and unbuckle yourself too." When the brushes started down the back window, he grabbed the diaper bag and swung around, scooping up RJ. He went out the driver's door with Jackie close behind him. He was grateful he didn't have to drag her along. Water dripped on him and down his collar.

At the other end of the car wash was a fenced-in dumpster. He swung open the dumpster gates where he'd parked his motorcycle sometime before and grabbed the helmets for Jackie and RJ. Jackie put on hers, then RJ's while Roger stuffed the diaper bag in one of the leather saddlebags and donned his own helmet. "Get on the back." He didn't want to order her, but he also couldn't let her challenge him.

Jackie climbed on without question. He hoisted RJ up, then sat down in front of both of them. He pulled out and tried to keep the car wash between him and Sweeny. He drove around for awhile to make sure they weren't followed. Sweeny would be livid, but Jackie and RJ were safe—for now. *Lord, thank You for getting us this far safely. Keep us ahead of him until I can make an inside contact I can trust.*

He pulled into one of the low-end motels where he'd rented a room and parked behind the building. He led Jackie and RJ to the room farthest from the office and unlocked the door with one of the keys in his pocket. It wasn't a great place, but it was inconspicuous, and they wouldn't be staying long.

❧

RJ headed straight for the TV and patted the screen. "Mote?"

Jackie pulled the on button, and the box sparked to life, then hummed. She turned the channel knob to a PBS station, and RJ was content to stand a foot from the green cat walking along a fence. Everything was a sickly shade of green. No expense had been spared, she observed with disgust.

Roger stood at the window peering out, his gaze fixed on something enthralling. But what?

Jackie stepped over to the window and threw back the curtains. "Let the sunshine in!" It was cloudy outside. *No more so than inside,* she thought.

Roger yanked the curtains closed. "Don't do that!" That was the sharpest he had ever spoken to her.

But she wouldn't back down. "What's so interesting out

there? Hot babes? If you didn't want them to know you had a family, why drag us along?"

He shook his head in exasperation before she turned and crossed the room. She hadn't asked to come. She was an unwilling participant in this little oasis. *Lord, what is going on here? How can You expect me to trust him after this stunt?*

Other than the ancient TV, there were two double beds. She went to the far end of the room and set down the diaper bag, peeking into the bathroom. At least it was clean; even the rust stains in the sink sparkled.

She sat down on the edge of the bed closest to the bathroom and picked at a chipped nail, peeling it back to almost nothing. Roger had a gun! Was it to uphold the law or break it? Obviously he wasn't a consultant for anyone. But who was he? She could sit here and wonder or do something. She rose and grabbed the diaper bag. "I want to leave."

Roger left the window and strode toward her, hooking his arm around her waist as she crossed the room toward RJ. "I can't let you do that."

She stepped back from him. "Why not? Are we prisoners?"

"Of course not."

"Why then?"

He raked a hand through his dark hair. "Because there are people out there who wouldn't hesitate a moment to use you and RJ to get to me."

"Who?"

"The less you know, Jackie, the safer you and RJ will be."

"Safe? Are we safe?"

He sighed. "Of course you are, as long as you do what I tell you."

Was that a threat? "It seems we are already in about as much danger as we can be." It was a stab, but she didn't care. "Can you at least tell me if they are the bad guys"—she swallowed hard—"or the good guys?"

He hesitated. "Both." He returned to the window.

Did he mean the police were looking for him? For what? Who were the bad guys after him? And what did they want with him? So did this mean her husband was not only a marked man but a wanted man as well? The diaper bag slid off her shoulder and hit the floor with a thud.

ten

The green cat was gone, and RJ was no longer satisfied with watching TV. He arched his back and started crying. Jackie tried to soothe him. She caressed his back and sang softly to him. She didn't want to talk to Roger right now, let alone ask him for something. But tired and hungry were an unpleasant combination for her son. "RJ's hungry."

Roger turned from his vigil at the window. "There's a bag of food in the corner."

She found it and pulled out a box of graham crackers, a package of beef jerky, and a bag of apples. Down at the bottom were some juice boxes and a couple of cans of Vienna sausages, little "hot dogs" in a can. Roger had been thinking of his son when he bought this food. She also discovered two adult toothbrushes, a child's toothbrush with a dinosaur handle and her brand of toothpaste along with some deodorant. He had thought of everything before he went to her house and kidnapped them. Everything was neatly planned.

She took a juice box and opened a can of sausages. RJ gobbled them down while she chewed on some jerky. She would have to remember how much he liked these mini hot dogs and buy him some when they got home— Would they ever go home again? she wondered. And where was Roger taking them?

He said people would use her and RJ to get to him. She didn't want to be used. She just wanted her life back to normal. But when had it last been normal?

RJ lay down on the bed with his motorcycle tucked under his arm and watched dancing green bugs on a green stage with green tomatoes being thrown at them. It wouldn't be long before he fell asleep from exhaustion. He hadn't been getting the sleep he needed since Roger had reappeared. Neither had she.

Why was Roger doing this? Because someone was after him? But who? She hadn't seen anyone. Was it a phantom enemy? She hadn't known Roger that well when she married him. She thought she had a lifetime to get to know him. Roger was only strengthening her parents' suspicions by his current actions. When they found out about this, they would hit the roof. She should call them to let them know she and RJ were safe—more or less. She crossed the room to the phone and picked up the receiver and began to dial.

Roger pressed the button. "You can't call anyone."

"My parents will be worried."

"I left a note."

"When?"

"With the balloons. It was to you, asking you to go away with me for a few days, but I'm sure they'll read it."

"You thought of everything."

"It doesn't pay to be careless."

He said a few days in the note, but they hadn't left town. "When can we go back home?"

"A few days."

Was everything a vague answer with him? "How many? Two? Three?"

"I don't know. Maybe a week."

"I can't miss a whole week of work!"

"I'm sorry it has to be this way. Just trust me."

"Trust! You take us out of the house at gunpoint, and you expect me to trust you?"

"I did not point my gun at you."

"You might as well have." She was beginning to sound like her mother when she exaggerated.

She stalked over to the corner between the wall and the far bed, sat down, and closed her tired eyes. How had things come to this? What kind of drama were they acting out? She felt the danger Roger spoke of all right but strangely not from him. Why not? He was the one with the gun. Could she believe what little information he had given her? If both the good guys and the bad guys were after him, then what did that make him? Was he a good guy gone bad? Or a bad guy gone good? She wasn't sure she wanted to know or was ready for the answers. Was this all for real or some elaborate scheme? Just because Roger had a gun and he said people were after him didn't make it true. What if he was mentally ill and this was a delusion?

It was all too much. She pushed herself up from the floor, slipped into the bathroom, and locked the door behind her.

After a few minutes, she could hear him walk across the room and stop outside the door.

"Jackie?"

"What?"

"I need to know you're still in there."

"Are you crazy? Why would I leave? You have my son!"

"I don't have him. You're both here with me. I just want to make sure you don't get any ideas about leaving."

"So tie my ankles together."

"I don't have any rope, and even if I did I wouldn't use it on you."

Was that supposed to make her feel better?

"Jackie?"

She suppressed the urge to reply. He would just have to trust her. She heard him walk away from the door.

She sat on the floor and sobbed into her hands.

❧

Roger had heard the water turn off and expected Jackie to emerge at any minute. But she hadn't. He knew the window in the bathroom was large enough to crawl through. After all, he'd chosen the room with that in mind. He had also heard her crying and almost asked if he could comfort her in any way, but he suspected she would refuse. He knew he was the likely cause. He would finish his job, then he could focus on his family and work at getting them back. Jackie would understand in the end. He had to believe that. Otherwise what hope was there? God was his hope, though, and He alone would see them through.

He could smell his son's diaper from across the room. RJ had awakened a few minutes earlier and patted the TV to get him to turn it on. Something had to be done about the diaper. Jackie had changed more than her share. It was his turn now. He laid RJ on the bed, but the little boy twisted and turned to keep the TV in sight. Roger moved him so he could still see the green characters on the old set, then grabbed the diaper bag. He was hunting for a clean diaper when the bathroom door opened.

"What are you doing?" Jackie all but screamed as she hurried across the room and yanked the diaper bag from his hand.

He had hold of a diaper so several articles fell out of the bag when she pulled it away. "I was changing my son's diaper. He needs a new one."

"I'll do it." Her face was streaked with tears.

What was her problem? What was she afraid of? "I'm capable of changing a diaper."

"Have you ever changed one before?"

Was she glaring at him? "I don't think it's that difficult."

She stared at him, defiant, for long frozen seconds. Suddenly she started grabbing items out of the diaper bag. "You have to put this under him." She handed him a folded plastic pad. "Use these to clean him." She dropped a long blue plastic case labelled wipes next to RJ.

If he and Jackie couldn't find a better way to relate to each other, maybe for RJ's sake he shouldn't be around much. No, two loving parents were always best. Once he could tell her everything, then maybe she would trust a little and not get so disturbed over something as simple as his changing his son's diaper. She had reservations about him, justifiably so. He would be patient with her until this was all over and settled. Then they could sit down and try to talk everything out rationally.

Then again, perhaps he should grab her and kiss her until her reservations about him were gone. That wouldn't likely happen, but a guy could have his fantasy.

"What are you smiling about? Is something funny?"

"Nothing." He didn't think she would appreciate his thoughts.

Jackie put the diaper bag on the floor away from him and watched every move he made. She obviously didn't trust him to do it right.

Lord, help me to show Jackie she can trust me. Let her see I was trying to keep her from harm and never meant to hurt her.

&

Jackie tried her best to ignore Roger, but it wasn't easy when he was in her every thought. Roger was chewing on a piece of beef jerky and seemed to be sulking. Okay, so she was the one sulking, not him. He was just sitting near the window in a chair, tipped back against the wall with his eyes closed. She shouldn't have reacted so strongly. It was just so startling to find Roger with RJ and the diaper bag. He was invading her belongings, her private possessions, without asking. He had no right to pry and snoop.

"Time for bed." Roger's voice shattered her daze.

She picked up RJ and made for the bed farthest from Roger's window vigil. "We'll sleep here."

"Not if I'm going to get any sleep. You can have that bed to yourself." He walked over to her and held out his arms for RJ.

She held onto him. "Why can't RJ sleep with me?"

"Unless I have one of you close at hand I won't sleep. And I didn't figure you would volunteer to share a bed with me."

She handed RJ over.

"Sleep with your clothes and shoes on."

"My shoes?"

"Just in case."

"Just in case what?" She gave her head a tight shake. She didn't want to know.

After they were all settled into bed, one small voice rose in the darkness. "Mama."

Jackie wanted to hold him. "It's okay. Mommy's here." She could hear covers rustling.

"Settle down now." Roger's words were no comfort.

"Mamaaaa!"

"RJ, go to sleep. Mommy's right over there. It's okay."

She could hear the struggle. You couldn't rationalize with a two year old.

RJ began to cry, louder and louder.

She slipped out of bed and knelt on the floor next to the other bed and tried to soothe RJ with a caressing hand. He strained harder to get to her.

Finally Roger rolled to his back, releasing RJ. "My son's afraid of me."

RJ gripped her so tight he was nearly choking her, but his sobbing subsided. "He's not used to you. And he's overtired." Those words would have to be enough for him.

She could hear Roger get out of bed; then she saw light from the window and his silhouette. She lay down on her bed with RJ and calmed him. Every once in awhile he would shudder. Her eyes had grown accustomed to the dark. She wanted to comfort her husband as well, but she just lay there. The conflict inside pulled her in opposite directions. She watched Roger move from the window to the chair he had propped under the doorknob. He sat in it and leaned against the door. He wasn't actually going to sleep in that chair? But if he didn't he couldn't keep either one of them "close at hand."

RJ's breathing was steady. She tried to sleep, but her eyes refused to stay shut. She would close them, but they would spring back open with every little noise, real or not. She heard Roger move in the darkness. The bed dipped, and she could feel him curl up behind her. The covers pulled tight over her as he lay on top of them. He draped an arm over her waist. She sucked in a breath and went stiff.

"I just want sleep. I'll wake up if you try to leave," he whispered near her ear. And soon his breathing was steady too.

She didn't dare move but forced her eyes to close. She wanted sleep too.

Jackie woke from her dream to hear steady thumping against her ear and a warmth like a blazing fire still there. It was comforting. At the growl of Roger's stomach, she jerked up onto her hands away from her toasty, comfortable illusion and stared down at him.

His eyes were coaxing her back as he tugged gently on her shoulders. "Please—I want to hold you. To pretend everything is back the way it was—for a little while."

She wanted to forget everything and lie in her husband's arms and pretend all was right and normal too. Her own heart betrayed her. How could she want to be here with this stranger? After all he had done. All she didn't know. And how could she still love him? Their lives were some sort of lie, and yet her heart wanted to be beating next to his. If he knew how weak and vulnerable she was to him, would he use it against her?

"You'll wake RJ," Roger whispered.

Her muscles relaxed, and she was against his chest again. He had spoiled it. But they both got what they wanted. If he thought her motive was simply not to disturb RJ, that was okay. It made it easier than letting him know he was getting to her.

His light squeeze was a thank-you.

Love was a peculiar thing. It made no sense at all and was impossible to tame. Even now with all this, she wanted—wanted!—to be here in his arms. He seemed to want to protect her and keep her safe even without the envelope. She was more important. Or was it all a hoax? As strange as it seemed, this was where she wanted to be—with Roger—wherever. Her heart beating in sync with his. How? How could that be? How could she betray herself like that?

≫

Later that morning, Roger sensed deep inside the familiar warning for him to flee. "Time to go," he told Jackie.

She quickly gathered her belongings and her son and preceded him out the door.

He grabbed her arm and turned her to face him. The seemingly pleasant expression on her face confused him, and his insides stirred. What was she up to? Had she had a change of heart toward him? Or was she planning to escape?

"Please don't run, Jackie."

"I won't." Her voice was eerily calm and quiet.

He scrutinized her. What was she up to? He might be able to figure it out if he weren't distracted by the other feelings she caused in him. He had to stay focused to keep them all safe and alive.

He pulled into the next low-end motel where he had rented a room. They couldn't stay in one place very long. He couldn't give Sweeny the opportunity to track him and catch up to them. He wished he could do better for her, but they had to stay inconspicuous and have more than one way out. The fewer people who saw them, the better.

He let Jackie go about the room caring for RJ's needs while he kept an eye out for unwanted visitors. It was best that way. So far no one had caught up to them. He only had to keep this up for a few more days. He would meet his contact, Troy Peppermill, tomorrow to get things rolling and hoped the man wasn't playing for the wrong team. That was the mistake Moore had made. Trusting one wrong man. No black or white hats to tell the bad from the good. And they easily deserted given the right encouragement or a bullet.

❧

Jackie's head was throbbing. She sat on the corner of the bed nearest the bathroom, rubbing her temples. Roger stood in front of the mirror; he had finished shaving and was reaching for his shirt. She let her gaze wander to his bare back. She sucked in a quick breath at the sight of a round pucker of skin on his right shoulder. Only one thing made a scar like that. Roger spun around. She stood and gasped at the matching scar on the front of his chest. She extended her hand slowly and touched it. "The bullet went clear through."

The scar was old and well healed. "When?"

His jaw tightened. "Call it an anniversary present."

Suddenly it all crashed in on her. Maybe he had been telling her the truth. Was someone really after him? She let her finger slide down to his side where a long, jagged scar meandered around to his back. It was fresh and still pink. "What's this one from?"

He sucked in a controlled breath as he worked his jaw. "A piece of scrap metal I failed to dodge." He seemed to be having trouble breathing.

She traced the scar. "You didn't have these before."

"No, I didn't." Roger grasped her hand. "Please don't do that."

Startled, she looked up. "I wouldn't think it still hurt."

"It doesn't. I'm just finding it difficult for you to touch me."

Her insides flipped. She saw her husband as she once had, with the clutter and pain of the last two-and-a-half years dissolved. "Why did you leave me?"

"To keep you safe."

She cupped his face with her free hand. He leaned into her touch. Slowly he moved closer to her, inch by inch. She slid her hand around to the back of his neck, and his approach hastened. Their lips connected, and she felt it was right to be here with Roger. He was her husband, and she belonged with him for better or for worse.

Suddenly a terrified voice cried out. "Mama!"

She turned. "I'm here, RJ."

Roger returned to his watch post. The spell had been broken.

Again she slept with RJ nestled against her stomach and Roger her back. And she woke draped across Roger's chest again. This time she didn't move. Roger didn't say anything, but she sensed he knew she was awake. She could see his scars in her mind. A bullet wound. The bloody cell phone. The recent gash on his side. It must have been awful for him. What was he mixed up in?

❧

Roger pulled up to the curb across the street from the corporate headquarters of ICOM Electronics with Jackie and RJ behind him on the motorcycle. He had wanted to leave them at the motel, leave them out of this. If he were sure they'd be safe and would still be there when he returned, he would have. He'd had to weigh the risk of bringing them here with the risk of not. Neither was good. Jackie and RJ used to be safe without him. Now they were in danger with or without him. At least with him he would know when danger lurked nearby.

He watched the building. A tall, slender fellow in his twenties wearing a dark suit stepped out of the ICOM building and crossed the parking lot to the southwest corner. This could be his man. He would know soon enough. The man looked around, anxious about something. If he was the one, he should be anxious. This was a dangerous game. The man looked up and down the street and scanned the parking lot, then walked back into the building.

If that wasn't his man, where was he? *Come on, Troy Peppermill. Where are you?* Without the CD he needed someone on the inside more than ever. It wasn't easy to trust a stranger with your life and the lives of your family.

The man in the dark suit reappeared twisting a blue baseball hat in his hands. *So maybe you are Troy.* When the man reached the southwest corner again, he straightened the hat and punched his hand into it.

Come on. If you're Troy, make up your mind to play or not and put it on.

The man rubbed a hand back and forth over his mouth and pulled the hat snug on his straight, brown hair; a big white M for Mariners stood out on his head. The signal it was safe.

Roger drove down the street and U-turned at the next light. He pulled up to the ICOM building on the west side where the building met the street and parked his motorcycle at the curb. He glanced around and walked close to Jackie carrying RJ as they moved alongside the ICOM building to the parking lot side. Jackie had been quiet and compliant ever since they'd left the motel. But he felt an undercurrent. What was going on inside her head? Did she sense his tension? Was she scheming something? He had to trust she wouldn't bolt on him.

Two older men approached Troy. Roger stopped and put his arm in front of Jackie to keep her from taking another step. He pressed them all against the side of the ICOM building out of the direct line of sight of the three men.

No! If those two men were who Roger believed them to be, they suspected Troy was helping him. Troy must have been careless, and they'd caught him. Troy had been his best hope.

Roger's whole body tensed like an over-wound rubber band ready to snap. Should he wait until the men left? Or run now? He needed Troy to finish this. He took a couple of calming breaths to clear his head.

Troy removed the hat and tapped it on his thigh. That was surely a sign not to approach. The men pointed to the hat, asking about it. Not company issue, Roger could imagine their saying. Troy pointed to the dark sky. Looks like rain, Troy would reply. Roger hoped they didn't ask him whom he was meeting. He couldn't chance Troy's slipping up or one of them turning around to see him.

Roger backed his family up and made a quick departure. One of those men, he was sure, was Fillmore, Sweeny's keeper. They'd already killed Moore. Troy could be next if they suspected he was meeting him to pass him information. They would watch him more closely. But as long as they thought they could track Roger through Troy, he'd be safe—for now.

But had Troy been compromised? Would he change sides? Could he be bought? Roger would try to contact Troy tomorrow.

eleven

Roger had passed down this corridor before. The doors too close together. Escape impossible. A dark cloud closing in. Run! He took off down the endless hall of doors. RJ cried from behind one of the doors. He skidded to a stop. Which one? He tried a door but couldn't open it. He rammed his shoulder into it. He tried another and another. RJ cried from behind each one. None of them would open. The dark cloud spread and grew closer. Like hot breath on his neck.

"I'll come back for you, Son. I promise." He ran on.

Jackie called to him. He stopped again and banged on the door. "Open the door."

She kept calling his name. "Roger, help me."

"Open the door!"

"I can't."

He knew she could. The door opened from the inside. They all did. The darkness intensified and reached out for him. He ran again. RJ and Jackie cried and called to him from behind every door. The grotesque shadow had nearly overtaken him. He had to keep running or Jackie and RJ would be in peril. "I'll be back. I promise. I'll come back for both of you." He would run until they were safe.

"Wake up."

Roger woke in a sweat.

Jackie caressed his arm. "It's just a dream. Shhh." Her voice was slurred and still half asleep.

"I'm awake." Another bad dream she had to wake him from. How many times had she done that in their marriage? He took his Glock from under the pillow and rolled off the bed. Stepping to the window, he pulled the curtain back a crack. The parking lot was still, the street quiet. Three A.M. He was finished with sleep for the night. RJ had never been in that nightmare before! His son had never been so real to him before.

Troy Peppermill with Fillmore. Had he been compromised? Would he change sides? He had no way of telling. Troy was still his best bet at this point. But how could he contact him with an unwilling wife and toddler in tow? If he could be sure they would stay put, he would leave them behind. He would try to contact Troy tomorrow—or later today. Now that he knew what the man looked like, he could catch him off-guard, maybe at the grocery store or walking his dog if he had one.

Jackie joined him at the window and reached in her pocket, pulling out a coin. "I don't have a penny, but I have a quarter." She spoke softly. Though she didn't mean to, her voice had a husky rasp to it.

He let the curtain drop and looked from the quarter to her face. "I was just thinking about Moore." He kept his voice low too.

"Mr. Moore, your boss?"

He nodded. "He was more a friend than a boss. We went to college together. People always mixed us up or mixed up our names. I got called Roger Moore a number of times. Ironic. We even sat in on each other's classes. We looked enough alike that the professors either didn't notice or didn't care."

"Does Mr. Moore have a mole on his cheek?" She touched her left cheek.

How would she know that? She'd never seen him. "Yes." He heard her labored breaths.

"Where is he—now?"

"He's dead." It was hard for him to admit.

She gasped. "Our anniversary?"

"Yes."

She acted as if she was going to sit down, but no chair was behind her. He grabbed her upper arms and held her up. "Jackie, what is it?"

She struggled not to cry but was losing the battle. "I saw him. In the morgue."

He pulled her to him and held her. "I'm sorry."

"I didn't know it was him." She shook her head into his chest. "They thought it was you. It was awful."

"I'm so sorry."

"I never knew his first name."

"Jim."

She lifted her head off his chest. "You said you were still working for him. How?"

"I'm finishing what we started. He's dead because I refused to pull out. He was eager to get these guys too. But if I had pulled the plug, it all would have stopped. He'd have left the company and still be alive."

"So you're doing this to avenge his death or something?"

"I'm in too deep now to pull out. They know about me— and you. I was stupid to think I could protect you. I didn't know how big this was when I met you. Maybe if I had focused more attention on this job instead of always thinking about you, I could have finished this sooner and Moore would still be alive. I didn't want to lose you, but it was wrong to get married while I was working on this."

Jackie pushed away from him and slapped both hands on his chest.

He grabbed her wrists. "Wait."

"Leave me alone. I'm just a mistake in your life."

"No, no, you're not. You and RJ are the only right things in my life next to God." Though she struggled, he held her against him. *Lord, what more should I say to her?*

The truth.

He knew. "Jackie, you're not a mistake. Marrying you was

right." He took a deep breath. "Where I went wrong was this job." She stilled in his embrace. "The Lord urged me not to get involved. I chalked it up to my being restless. I wanted to help Moore. I thought I could handle it. I should have pulled out the day I met you. I'm so sorry for everything."

He held her for a long time. It felt good to have her against him. He kissed the top of her head and the side, her temple and down her cheek until he found her mouth. He was tentative at first, but she responded.

She disengaged her lips and snuggled up to his chest. Holding her again felt so right. What was she thinking? He knew where his thinking would lead, and he had to stop now. It was already hard enough being so close to her and not giving in to his desires. He would be content with what he had for now.

She pulled away. "I'm going back to bed. Are you?"

He touched her cheek and caressed her hair. "No, you go ahead." He watched her climb back into bed next to his son. He marveled that he had a son! It still amazed him.

With the way Jackie responded to his kiss earlier, then again a few minutes ago, he had real hope for their future together. He had to stop thinking about her that way or he would go crazy. It was much safer thinking about Moore and how he'd let his friend down. That would drive him crazy too.

Moore had suspected it had been a trap, but Roger thought they could handle it and end it once and for all. It had ended for his friend, all right. But Roger's torture lingered on. Sensing the danger looming on the horizon, Moore had given him the CD earlier that day.

He walked to the bed. Jackie's even breathing told him she was asleep. He touched her silky brown hair fanned out on the pillow, then stepped into the bathroom to shower away the sweat and fatigue.

❧

Jackie lay on her back and stared at the red light blinking on the smoke detector attached to the ceiling. She listened to the water running in the shower. She was sure Roger thought she was asleep before leaving her unattended. What was going on with him? She had seen no tangible evidence of his troubles. Except his word and his scars. Was that enough? Or was it an elaborate scam? He could have acquired those scars anywhere and was only claiming someone was after him. She didn't know what to think. It was all so unbelievable. She wanted to trust him, but he was still keeping things from her. Was this like one of those wild stories on "That's Incredible"? Could she believe everything Roger told her? Or had she been swindled by a master con?

This was her chance to run. She should get up, grab RJ and the diaper bag, and leave. The covers felt heavy, pinning her down. The light blinked on the ceiling. The water ran. RJ breathing deeply. Her racing heart. Everything seemed exaggerated. The light. The water. The breathing. Her heart. *Thump, thump. Thump, thump.* The water shut off. *Thump, thump.* Blink. Breathe. *Thump.* Blink. Breathe—

Lord, help me.

I'm here.

What should I do?

You already know.

Trust? But how? I don't know how. Please show me.

The bathroom door opened, and Roger crossed the room.

Would he come back to bed or sit in the chair and wait? He checked out the window, then sat in the chair by the door. After a few minutes, he checked the window again and sat. He kept checking and sitting. Was this proof of his restlessness? She drifted off to sleep.

"Wake up!"

Jackie woke to find Roger standing over her, his eyes wide with panic. He threw back the covers and pulled her up to a sitting position.

Fear gripped her. "What's wrong?"

"We have to leave—now!" Roger lifted RJ into his arms and grabbed her wrist, pulling her behind him. He released her and opened the door a crack. They inched out and around the side of the building.

She caught a glimpse of a man in a dark coat searching for something—or someone. Her own panic rose to paralyzing proportions. Was that who Roger was running from? Roger pulled her along after him.

Behind the motel she barely had time to secure RJ's helmet before Roger set the motorcycle in motion. He drove around town, across one bridge and back on the other. He made one stop for gas and drove again. He finally stopped at a motel in Bellevue across Lake Washington from Seattle. Once inside he stood at the window, peering out between the curtains.

Jackie set RJ on the bed and headed for the door. "I left the diaper bag. We have to go back and get it."

Roger grabbed her elbow to stop her escape. "No, Jackie. Consider it gone."

"No, we have to get it!" She tried to pull away.

He steadied his grip on her. "It's just a diaper bag. We can buy another one."

He didn't understand. She twisted to free herself. "It has stuff in it."

Roger backed her up and pressed her against the wall, pinning her shoulders. "It's not safe. We'll replace it all. Let go of the diaper bag. Don't fall apart on me now."

She stopped fighting. "Not everything can be replaced." She let her head fall back against the wall. "Oh, Roger. I'm so sorry. I wanted to know what was more important to you than me."

He stared at her in silence.

"My sitter's teenage son is a whiz with computers. I thought he might be able to help me figure out the password. It seemed like a logical place. I always have RJ's bag with me. I thought it was safe." She could see understanding slowly nudging out the confusion and questions.

"No, Jackie. You didn't." He rocked his head back and forth. "You had it this whole time and kept it from me?"

She managed a slight nod. She had to hold onto it. It was all she had.

His eyebrows knit together in shock and disbelief. "Why, Jackie? Why?"

Tears welled up in her eyes. She shook her head. "You wouldn't tell me anything."

"No wonder you got bent out of shape when I was changing RJ's diaper. It wasn't the diaper but the stupid bag." His grip on her shoulders tightened. "You knew it was important to me."

"Yeah, more important than I am. I was afraid you would leave again. Isn't it the reason you came back? Once you had it, what would stop you from vanishing again?"

"Yes, I came for the CD but not so I could leave again—so I could stay!" He released her and walked across the room. "The information on that CD not only will put a good many people behind bars, but it will clear me. I'll be able to stop running."

"I'm so sorry." It was lame, but she didn't know what else to say.

He sat on the end of the bed, raked his hands through his hair, and held his head. She had seen him like this before. He was thinking and worried.

Did he hate her? She covered her mouth with her hand. *Please, Lord, don't let me have ruined everything. Fix my mistake.*

"James 1:1."

She took an unsteady breath. "What?"

Roger raised his head. "The password. James 1:1. 'James,

a servant of God and of the Lord Jesus Christ.' Moore picked the password."

So she never would have figured it out. "Can't we go back for the bag? Surely whoever was there is gone by now."

"And they have the CD too."

"Maybe not." She went over and knelt on the floor in front of him. "Would they have taken the bag or just searched it?"

"Why?"

"Well, I figure they would search the bag. The only reason to take the bag is if they thought the CD was in it. And if they thought that, they would take it. So if the bag is still there, the CD probably is too."

"And you don't think they would have found it when they dumped the bag and searched all the pockets?"

"They could have missed it. I hid it."

Roger put his hands gently on her shoulders. "They have it."

"I hid it in the bottom cardboard thing where there's a hole."

"What are you talking about?"

"In the bottom of the bag is a piece of plastic-covered cardboard that makes the bottom stay flat. There's a tear in one end of the plastic. I slipped the CD in there, and the cardboard piece sticks to the bottom of the diaper bag because juice spilled in it. It looks like the bottom of the bag. They would probably have no reason to take it out, and it wouldn't likely fall out even if they dumped the bag."

Roger was silent as he stared at her and tried to understand what she had said.

"Come on—I'll show you."

He held her in place. "I'll go. I need you and RJ to stay here." He looked resigned to his fate. Did he think he wasn't coming back? "Promise me you'll stay put."

"I promise." Tears streamed down her cheeks.

"This isn't a game. These guys play for keeps."

"I know." It had taken her a long time to believe someone was indeed after him—them.

"I will be back. I promise. I won't leave again without you and RJ. Once I turn the CD over to the authorities, we'll have to lie low while they round everyone up."

She nodded. "If only I had trusted you."

"I didn't make it easy for you." He pulled her close and kissed her before he left.

Lord, protect Roger and keep him safe.

Jackie turned to the bed where RJ was lying on his side, sucking his thumb. When she looked at him, he stood and held one arm and an elbow out to her with his thumb securely in his mouth. She picked him up and felt the toy Harley tangle in her hair.

"Hungee," RJ said around the thumb in his mouth.

Jackie located the bag of provisions and found some applesauce cups. She bibbed him in a towel from the bathroom, opened one of the cups, and gave it to him. RJ sat on the floor and spooned out the applesauce hungrily.

Jackie sat on the bed and leaned against the headboard. Something reminded her of the women's retreat she'd attended last month. The theme of the weekend was trust. One of the speaker's talks was on trusting your husband. She thought she had until he came back. Since then, everything regarding Roger was confusing. The speaker said to trust that your husband had your best interests at heart. Did he? Could she really trust Roger completely after all the hurt and pain he'd caused her? No. But she could trust God to get her and RJ out of this situation safely. But Roger? God chose him. . .put him over you, the speaker had said. God wasn't asking her to trust Roger but to trust Him. Roger wasn't in charge here. God was and always had been. *Lord, I do trust You. And I trust You will get us all out of this safely.* A peace and a hope she couldn't understand washed over her.

RJ came up to her with an unopened applesauce cup. "Nudder one."

Jackie opened it, and he went back to his spot on the floor to eat it. Finally she could trust Roger because she trusted God. He was telling her the truth, and everything made sense, even the things she didn't know.

Oh, Father God. I've only been going through the motions of Christianity. Attending church. Reading the Bible. But none of it sank in. It just bounced off the surface of my life. I haven't even felt alive these past two and a half years. Drifting from one day to the next, doing it all on the outside but inside hiding the emptiness.

For the first time in ages, she wanted to read the Bible, not out of duty or obligation, but to be fed and comforted. She opened the nightstand drawer and, bless the Gideons, found a Bible. Not knowing where to go, she flipped it open to Psalm 20 and read. Each verse struck her as new and poignant. When was the last time she felt the Word speaking directly to her, to her needs?

She couldn't just sit around this dingy motel and do nothing. She should take RJ and find a place to hide until Roger had retrieved the CD and given it to the authorities. They would be looking for Roger, not her. Couldn't Roger hide and move more easily on his own? She scooped up RJ and the bag of food. But how was this trusting God or Roger? What if the men out to get Roger found her? Her breathing came in short little puffs. She should stay and wait. She stared at the door trying to decide. This was stupid. She had no clue where to go to hide. She set RJ on the bed and turned on the TV.

She started at the frantic banging on the door.

"Jackie, open up! Hurry!"

She rushed to the door and fumbled with the chain. She pulled it off and turned the knob. The force on the door pushed her backward. She gasped. It wasn't Roger.

twelve

It was still early, and the traffic was light. Roger made it to the motel in good time. He pulled into the parking lot. It was mostly quiet except for a few early risers hefting their suitcases into the trunks of their cars. The door to the room they had occupied stood slightly ajar. *Please let the bag still be there with the CD.* He drove around back and parked. He drew his gun and made his way slowly around the end of the building. He took a deep breath before nudging the door open all the way. The room was empty, but he checked it anyway to be sure.

The contents of the diaper bag and Jackie's purse were scattered across the beds. He grabbed the empty diaper bag and looked in. Nothing. He looked closer. Jackie was right. The flat bottom did look like part of the bag. He wedged his fingers under one edge and pulled up. The plastic-covered cardboard came loose with a sort of snapping noise. Juice was obviously a good adhesive. He found the slit and pulled out the envelope encased in a zipped-up baggie. The CD was tucked safely inside. Now he would see that everyone responsible paid for Moore's death. He wouldn't stop until every last one of them was brought down. He owed it to Moore to nail as many as possible.

A verse entered his thoughts. "Do not take revenge, my friends, but leave room for God's wrath, for it is written: 'It is mine to avenge; I will repay,' says the Lord."

I'm still doing it, aren't I , Lord? I've taken back this quest into my own hands. I started this battle. You didn't authorize it, and I've kept at it at great personal sacrifice. I need to know all who are responsible will get what is due them.

Another verse came to mind. "Be sure of this: The wicked will not go unpunished."

He shook his head. *This was never my fight. You only wanted me to trust You for justice in this. I have held onto this for so long. How do I let go? I can't trust our justice system not to mess things up when it lets criminals slip through.*

Trust Me! And yet another verse came to encourage him. "The Lord is slow to anger and great in power; the Lord will not leave the guilty unpunished."

Okay, Lord. I'll turn over the CD and trust You to take care of the rest. Even if all the guilty ones aren't caught in this world, You'll deal with them in the next. He paused. *Even if no one is caught, I'll trust Your will to be done.* The lightness in his soul was like nothing he had ever felt. He had given the situation over to God before—or at least he thought he had. But now he knew it was in God's hands, and the outcome was in His control and would be fine.

He holstered his Glock and collected the contents of the diaper bag and Jackie's purse. His newfound peace was strange. Now to get Jackie and RJ and go to the authorities. He climbed on his bike and turned onto the street. He took the most direct route back to the motel but made sure no one was following. As soon as he slipped inside the door, he knew something was terribly wrong. The silence was eerie. He pulled out his gun and moved slowly through the room.

Jackie and RJ were nowhere. Where had they gone? Why hadn't she stayed? He pulled the CD from his pocket. "What do I do with you now?" he asked, staring at it.

He leaned on the dresser. "No, Jackie. You promised. We were so close. Please not back home. Were the looks and the words and the feelings just to gain my trust so you could escape?"

Something in the mirror caught his eye. He turned to the bed and plucked RJ's toy Harley from between the rumples in the bedspread. RJ wouldn't leave this willingly. Would Jackie have taken it from RJ because she was mad at him? She didn't seem mad when he left. Even so, she would have let RJ keep it. So why would the toy be here but not them? *No, Lord. Not that.*

He raced for the door. He would find them and rip Sweeny's heart out if he harmed either one of them. As he pulled the door shut, the phone rang. He jammed the room key into the lock and picked up the phone before the third ring.

"I've got your wife and boy. Sit tight. I'll be in touch."

He stumbled back to the bed. He should have taken them with him. He never should have left them here unprotected. How could he be so stupid? Moore was dead because of him and now Jackie and RJ. When would he learn? He paced back and forth in the room like a tiger in a cage. The walls were narrow and confining. But this room was bigger than the space Sweeny had given him after their encounter in California. He touched the side with the jagged scar.

He hit the wall with his fist. Why hadn't he taken his family and left town? They could have started over somewhere with new names. Why? Because he had to see this thing to the end, make sure justice was served. It had become revenge for him—and Jackie and RJ its victims.

&

Jackie held RJ close to her side in the front seat of the car. The man steered the car through the streets with one hand and held his gun against RJ's back with the other. Her only comfort was that if he pulled the trigger the bullet would go through her son and kill her too. This man would kill them both if she gave him trouble. She was sure of it. And now Roger's fear had come to pass. She and RJ were being used

against him. How could she have been so stupid? Roger had
the key. He wouldn't have called her to the door to open it.

The Lord would provide a way out of this, and even if He
didn't it would be okay. She had a strange peace. She would
wait for her opportunity and hope she had the courage to take
it when it came.

The man pulled in behind a grungy, run-down building.
"Get out."

She scooted out with RJ in her arms, jiggling him up and
down to soothe him. He was cranky and hungry. The man
ushered them up to the door. It was boarded and had a condemned sign on it. "Put him down and pull the boards loose."
He was slightly taller than Roger with hardly any meat on his
bones, certainly no muscle.

"I can't."

"You'd better, or I'll put you down here and save myself
some trouble." He pressed his gun to the back of her neck.

She wasn't ready to die yet and set RJ down next to her.
He cried and tried to climb up her. She forced herself to
ignore his pleas while she struggled with the boards.

"Shut him up!"

"I can't and get these boards off."

He grabbed the board she was pulling on and gave it a yank.
The board came free, and he twisted the knob. "Get inside!"

She picked up RJ and ducked between the boards. He pushed
her along the hallway. The spongy floor bowed beneath her.

"Shut him up."

"He's hungry and scared."

He raised his gun to RJ. "If you don't shut him up, I will."

She caressed his back. "Shhh, Honey. If you're quiet for
Mommy, I'll get you a whole box of cookies."

RJ continued to squirm and cry.

"I'll get you chocolate candy, if you're quiet for Mommy."

RJ sucked in a ragged breath. "Chocoe."

"Only if you are very, very quiet."

RJ tried his best not to make noise, but his breathing was still ragged and his voice whiny. "Chocoe now."

"No. When we leave, if you are very quiet." She held him close and kissed his head.

The man shoved her in the back. "Keep moving."

She was, but she walked a little faster. She didn't want to give him more of a reason than he already had to dispose of her. She passed a gaping hole in the wall to her right. She was approaching the front of the building. Certainly he didn't want her to go out the front.

He gripped her elbow hard, pinching it in his grasp, and turned her around the corner. "Go up."

She marched up the stairs and pushed open the fire door at the top. He pushed her to the right. She slowed toward the end of the hallway.

"In there." He guided her into a grimy apartment with water stains down the walls. Paper, rusty food cans, wood scraps, and other debris littered the floor, but at least it seemed solid. "Over there."

She walked to the wrought-iron room divider that sectioned off what must have been the living room from a small dining area. Tipped over in the corner was a broken, two-legged chair.

"Hug it." He motioned to the room divider.

She wrapped one arm around the room divider while keeping RJ in the other.

He handcuffed one wrist. "Things will go better for you and the boy if you cooperate with me."

She glared at him.

"Help me get the disc from Villeroy, and I'll let you and the boy live."

She doubted that. "What disc?"

"The one he was supposed to get from you. Give me your other wrist."

Was this her opportunity? She leaned down and set RJ on the floor. He protested, but she couldn't help it. She stood up fast and brought her fists under the man's chin, then swung out with her foot and kicked him in the shin. Scooping up RJ, she ran out of the room and down the hall and pulled open the fire door. She heard footsteps and the man cursing behind her. She rounded the corner at the bottom of the stairs and headed for the exit. Just as she reached it, the floor gave way, and she landed with one leg up to the knee through the rotting boards. RJ was sitting safely on the floor ahead of her. She heard the man's footsteps slow. She struggled to free herself, but the splintered wood dug into her flesh.

"I have half a mind to leave you there. But I have to go make a call, and you might free yourself." He stomped on the floor near the opening, careful not to fall through himself, and made the hole bigger. Grabbing her arm, he pulled her to her feet.

Pain raced through her calf as splinters stabbed her flesh. Through the rips in her jeans, she could see blood. She picked up RJ and hobbled at gunpoint back up the stairs and to the room with the wrought-iron divider. He cuffed her other wrist.

He rubbed his chin. "I won't forget this."

"Roger will come for us."

"I'm counting on it. But I hold all the cards. Villeroy's fate is sealed. As soon as he walks through the door, he's a dead man. I take the disc off him and dispose of the two of you." He ran a single finger down her cheek. "Too bad."

She didn't like the cold menacing look in his eyes and jerked her head quickly, biting down on his hand.

He howled and yanked his finger free, then pointed his gun at her. "I'm going to enjoy taking care of you. And don't think I'll be merciful." He stalked out.

She folded herself down into a sitting position, and RJ crawled onto her lap. "Shhh. Remember the chocolate." He whimpered in her arms, trying his best to be quiet.

At least now she knew she had the courage to take an opportunity when it came. She would crawl to her death if it freed RJ from this murderer's clutches. Her leg throbbed, and she prayed for strength to endure the pain.

&a.

Roger couldn't sit around the motel room doing nothing. He paced back and forth again. He had the CD but now couldn't turn it over to the authorities. It was his only bargaining chip. He would use it to rescue his family, then work on getting it back. He wished he could risk leaving and making a copy of it. Sweeny would give him no extra time to do that.

On the nightstand sat an open Bible. He picked it up and read Psalm 20. What had Jackie been reading? He flipped over to Daniel 3 and found comfort in the story of Shadrach, Meshach, and Abednego in the fiery furnace. *Lord, I know You are with Jackie and RJ wherever they are. Keep them safe in their fiery furnace.* He continued to read until the phone interrupted him. He jumped to answer it.

"I have what you want. Do you have what I want?"

"I want to talk to Jackie."

"Not possible. Do you have it?"

Not possible? That could mean a lot of things. They were still alive. They had to be. "Yes. Let's get this over with."

"First, the password. And don't give me something I can't use again."

He took a slow, deep breath. "James 1:1." He was hoping to hold onto that ace.

"You'd better be telling the truth." Sweeny gave him the address. "It will take you seventeen or eighteen minutes to get here. I'll give you twenty on account of morning traffic. If you're not here by then, all you'll find are two corpses. Oh, and don't even think of calling the police. Very bad for your family's health. The clock is ticking."

thirteen

Roger threw down the phone and raced for the door. He opened then closed it as quickly. Two men in an unmarked sedan—the Feds had found him too. He was slipping. He went to the bathroom, jimmied open the window, and jumped down next to his bike. It roared to life, and dirt spewed out behind him.

He was familiar with the neighborhood of the address Sweeny had given him. An abandoned building or warehouse no doubt. Sweeny couldn't be original. But he had no doubt the man would carry out his threat.

He turned right into the heavy morning traffic. Instead of squeezing between bumpers, he drove alongside the right lane. Sweeny knew it could easily take him twice as long as the time he allowed because of the morning rush. *Lord, show me the fast, clear route.*

He moved to the left lane and swerved between a white sedan and a green minivan. The sedan's horn blasted him. "I know—I'm sorry." Why was he apologizing? No one could hear him. Habit. He knew better. He wasn't driving this way on purpose. He hated it when people drove with no regard for the rules of the road. On a bike it was all the more dangerous. He hoped there were no cops in the vicinity.

If he took the Lakehills Connector, he might be able to shave off a little time. Every second counted. This was the right turn he needed to take. He cut off a blue pickup and was rewarded with a rude gesture. "Sorry." A steady line of cars wound down the hill. He followed the road down and up the other side. The left-turn lane had too many vehicles for them all to make it through, especially with a heavy construction truck in third place. He pulled out and drove on the yellow line up next to the lead car. In his head he could hear the kinds of comments being yelled at him and couldn't blame anyone.

One question kept coming back to him: How could he keep the CD and still free his family?

Let it go.

But all the account numbers. And I will look as guilty as the rest when this comes down. Sweeny would make sure of it. ICOM had already filed reports against him with the police.

Trust Me!

It's so hard to let this go. I don't know if I can. He thought of Paul in prison continuing his ministry, writing letters, and encouraging the church. And John was not hindered from writing Revelation when he was exiled to the island of Patmos. And Roger Villeroy would continue living for Jesus even if he was imprisoned. *Okay. It's Yours. I turn it over to You—again.*

The light turned green, and he darted off the starting line ahead of everyone.

☙

Jackie wanted to tell RJ to run away before the bad man got back, but she was afraid he would fall through the floor. He clung to her left leg. He probably wouldn't go even if she told him to.

She took hold of the wrought-iron bar and shoved it back and forth. The metal bowed, but she saw no sign of its coming free. She kicked the pole with her injured leg and winced. Searing pain bit her toes and seized her calf. She closed her eyes, clenched her teeth, and held her breath until the stabbing sensation subsided. She slumped to the floor on her good leg. RJ curled up against her with his head on her thigh and whimpered himself to sleep with an occasional ragged *chocoe*. She had to get him out of here.

Once again she gripped the bar with both hands and tugged. It didn't budge. The bolts in the ceiling and floor were secure. Her captor had found the one room where the floor wasn't rotting. She hit the bar with her palm in frustration and dropped her forehead against the cold metal. At least she didn't fear falling through the floor.

None of this had to happen. She should have trusted Roger from the start—instead of playing the wounded victim—believed someone was after him, and given him the CD. This was all her fault. Why had she insisted on playing this power-struggle game? She hadn't seen it as that until now.

At the sound of footsteps, she raised her head. Please be Roger. He didn't come in but instead walked around. Should she call to him? What if it wasn't Roger? He made too much noise to be Roger. She could hear splashing and the strong smell of gasoline.

A minute or so later, her captor appeared in the doorway, a satisfied grin on his face that she was still there. "Your soon-to-be-dearly-departed is on his way."

The news gave her no comfort. The man was setting a trap, and she and RJ were the bait. *There are those who would use you and RJ to get to me.* Roger's words haunted her.

He squatted down next to her and fondled her hair. "After I take care of Villeroy, I might let you convince me to keep the two of you alive."

"I would rather die."

"All part of the fun. But you might want to reconsider for the boy's sake." He glanced down at RJ.

"Let him go. He's too young to remember anything."

"In this decaying building? He might get hurt and suffer to death. I'll be doing him a favor." His cold penetrating blue gaze stabbed her heart.

She could never let that happen. *Lord, it doesn't matter what happens to me. Don't let RJ suffer and die.*

The man reached over and lifted RJ from her side. She wrestled for her son, grabbing hold of a piece of RJ's jeans. "Don't take him!"

He jerked RJ free from her grasp. "I need him to make sure Villeroy doesn't try any heroics." RJ struggled in his grasp and screamed.

She scrambled to her feet. "Take me instead."

He held RJ under one of his arms and around RJ's stomach. "This little guy will work better for what I have in mind."

"Wouldn't it be better to have us both to negotiate with?"

"There won't be any negotiations." He turned to walk out.

She pulled against her restraints. "Please take me. I'll do anything you want."

He turned back with his glacial blue eyes. "I know you will." He disappeared out of sight with her son. RJ's cries became more distant until she could no longer hear him.

She balanced on her good leg and yanked the handcuffs against the wrought iron. Maybe she could get the chain to break. She pushed and pulled on the divider, but it still wouldn't budge. Her wrists were red and bruised. Frustrated tears sprang to her eyes. She crumpled to the floor against the pole. "Take me." But she knew he could no longer hear her, and she cried.

❧

He was making good time despite the heavy traffic. Another green light. *Thank You, Lord.* He arrived miraculously with two minutes to spare and to assess his surroundings. He parked down the block so as not to forewarn Sweeny of his arrival. Indeed Sweeny had picked the cliché abandoned building, a dilapidated apartment house. If he simply wanted the

CD in exchange for Jackie and RJ's release, he would have chosen someplace open and public. But he wanted Roger dead and no witnesses to rat on him. So where else could he make the exchange in broad daylight and dispose of Roger and Jackie while still remaining anonymous? What if he had already harmed one or both of them? He clenched and un-clenched his fists at his side. Sweeny would regret it for the rest of his sorry life. He ought to go in there and— He took a deep breath to clear his mind and focus. He would be no good to Jackie and RJ if he rushed in on pure emotions.

Lord, guide and direct my steps. He remembered the verses in Psalms that had been his battle prayer for years. "I do not trust in my bow, my sword does not bring me victory; but you give us victory over our enemies, you put our adversaries to shame. In God we make our boast all day long, and we will praise your name forever." But this was the first time the beginning phrases of the verse struck him. His gun would not bring him victory. Only the Lord would. Never before had he viewed his Glock as insignificant. *The victory is Yours, Lord.*

He glanced at the front exterior door and shook his head—that was where he was supposed to enter. He circled around to the side and found a broken basement window. To have even a small element of surprise could be all he needed. He pulled his gun and climbed through the window. The pile of old newspapers he landed on was damp and made almost no noise. He could hear RJ's fervent crying, and his gut twisted. The smell of gasoline hung in the air. So Sweeny planned to burn their bodies in a condemned building fire. Not a bad tactic. Save the taxpayers a few dollars not to have to tear it down.

He crept up the stairs and was thankful none of them creaked. He slowly opened the door at the top of the stairs but stopped when it moaned. With RJ's persistent wailing, he doubted Sweeny heard it. He eased the door more slowly, enough to squeeze through. He came out at the intersection of two hallways. The doors down the long corridors seemed close together and weirdly reminiscent of his frequent nightmare. RJ's crying gripped his heart, wrenching it in two. *I'm coming, Son.*

Sweeny would be where he had a good view of the front entrance. Roger pointed his Glock in that direction and followed RJ's plaintive howling. The floor bowed slightly beneath him.

Most of the side wall of the front apartment was gone, and he had a clear view inside. The smell of gasoline was stronger here. Sweeny was on the far side of what was left of the room with a rope held tightly in his grasp, looking out a broken window. The man's gun was drawn and ready.

Roger crouched down. He had a clear shot and raised his gun.

Sweeny turned and looked up. "Shut up, you little brat! Your old man will be here real soon."

Roger looked up too, through the gaping hole in the wall. He adjusted his position until he could see RJ flailing from the other end of Sweeny's rope. It was tied around RJ's underarms. The ceiling in this apartment was also missing, and RJ dangled some twenty feet in the air.

He lowered his gun and put a palm to his forehead. Sweeny was getting more cunning. But where was Jackie?

"Come on, Villeroy! I haven't got all day!" Sweeny shouted.

Roger crept back down the hall to the opened door of the partial apartment. He could go through the apartment undetected and come up on Sweeny's blind side. But first a distraction so Sweeny wouldn't hear him coming.

He went back to the wall that mostly wasn't there.

"Your old man's late, Kid. I oughta shut you up for good."

"I'm here," he called through the huge opening but remained out of sight.

"So you snuck in the back way."

Not exactly.

"I was beginning to worry about you. Would hate for you to have gotten in a nasty accident."

I bet. "Where's Jackie?"

"Don't worry about her. You have more pressing matters. Do you have the disc?"

"I want to see Jackie first!"

"She's safe and sound in a cozy little upstairs apartment. The disc?"

He checked the magazine in his gun and holstered it. "Let my son go, and I'll give it to you."

"Give it to me, and I'll let him go."

He would like to give it to him. "Lower him first."

Sweeny let the rope go for a second and caught it again. RJ dropped a couple of feet and jerked to a stop. "Like that?"

Roger's heart stopped. RJ screamed.

Sweeny hoisted RJ back up.

"Okay. I'll give it to you." RJ had dropped only a couple of feet, but it was sudden. Regardless of the disc, he wouldn't let Sweeny get away with toying with his family.

"Come out where I can see you."

"So you can shoot me." He pulled the disc from his pocket.

"It's either you or him."

"You'll let him down easy once you have it?" Let Sweeny think he had him cornered and scared. He was scared but not for himself.

"Just give me the disc or he becomes part of the floor."

"I'm tossing it in." He held the envelope containing the CD like a Frisbee and gave his wrist a flick. *It's Yours, Lord.* It landed close enough to his mark. He hustled back down the hall and around the corner to the open apartment door then crept across the spongy floor.

Sweeny was bending over picking up the envelope. "You're a sucker, Villeroy. Come out where I can see you, or your boy comes down on express." Sweeny tucked the disc in his pocket.

Whatever you say. He rushed toward Sweeny, aiming for the rope. He rammed Sweeny in the side and took hold of the rope with one hand. The rope slid through his hand burning his palms. He grabbed hold with both hands and stopped RJ's descent.

Sweeny lost his footing. His gun spun on the floor and dropped down an open register vent. Roger swung around and clipped Sweeny in the head with his boot. He let the rope slide gently through his hands. RJ seemed mildly comforted by his presence but was still screaming.

Sweeny stood to his feet, blood dripping from his lip, and came at him. Roger tightened his grip on the rope. Sweeny broadsided him, knocking the air from Roger's lungs. Regardless he had to keep a tight hold of the rope. He struggled to draw a breath. Sweeny tried to pry the rope from his hand. He managed to push him off and inhale. As Sweeny stood to his feet and rushed at him again, Roger ducked and kicked him in the ribs. Sweeny sprawled on the floor, clutching his stomach.

Roger wrapped the rope around his left arm and grasped it with one hand. He reached in his coat and drew his gun. As Sweeny scampered like a rat through the doorway and out of sight, Roger squeezed off a shot. *Missed.*

৵

Jackie froze at the sound of a gunshot. "Rogerrr!" The sudden image of his healed bullet wound blinded her momentarily. *Don't let him be dead. I want another chance.*

She pulled on the cuffs until a trickle of blood rolled down onto her wrist. She stopped and watched her blood soak into her jeans. Was Roger bleeding to death somewhere in this building? Tears rolled down her cheeks, and her shoulders shook with silent sobs.

fourteen

Roger holstered his gun and lowered RJ hand over hand. "I've got you, Son." His precious son was in his arms again. RJ clutched him around the neck. *Thank You, Lord.* He loosened the slip knot at RJ's back and pried his son's little arms from around his neck long enough to pull the rope over his head. RJ clamped his arms back around his neck.

A sudden wall of flames *whooshed* to life on the other side of the gaping hole. "You can't save them both," Sweeny yelled above the roar.

Roger glanced at the hungry fire. Did he really have to choose? If he took RJ with him to search for Jackie, all three of them might perish. If he left RJ outside, at least he would live.

The smoke grew heavier. He tucked RJ into the front of his coat and covered his face. He had to find the clear path Sweeny had left for himself. He couldn't be so stupid as not to have thought of an escape route.

Out in the hall the smoke was thicker. He put his free arm over his mouth and nose. The bulk of the blaze was around the front door. He dashed in the opposite direction and caught his foot in a hole in the floor, nearly dropping RJ. He jerked his foot free and stayed close to the wall, testing the mushy floor as he went. The smoke burned his lungs, and he coughed.

He reached the back door. Though the door was open, boards were nailed across the frame. He raised a foot and broke two boards loose in the bottom half. Kicking again to clear them out of the way, he ducked through the doorway and down the steps.

Oh, Jackie. His heart pounded. His eyes watered. *I'll be back for you.*

A heavy mist blanketed the air. He knelt in the damp grass and opened his coat.

RJ looked up at him and blinked. "Chocoe?"

Roger shrugged. "I don't understand."

"JJ chocoe." His breathing was still ragged from so much crying, but he was safe.

"You stay here, Son." He looked back at the building, smoke pouring from it. He had to go back. Was Jackie even in there? He hadn't seen or heard any evidence of her. She could already be dead. Sweeny could have had her someplace else entirely. But he knew he had to search this place first. Once inside, he wouldn't likely come back out. He hoped the sacrifice wasn't for nothing.

RJ started back toward the building. "Mama."

Roger picked him up.

RJ started to cry again. "Want Mama. Want Mama!"

That was good enough for him. "You stay here, and I'll find Mommy." He set RJ back down.

RJ walked straight for the burning building again.

Roger picked him up once more. "You have to stay out here.

RJ held out a hand toward the building, crying. "Mama."

Precious seconds were being wasted! How could he make RJ understand? He couldn't go back in if RJ was going to follow him.

๛

The evil odor of smoke had replaced the smell of gasoline. She was going to burn to death! One shot. One dead. Roger? Or could it have been RJ? Had Roger even made it here? Which one? Her chest tightened. RJ! She couldn't hear him crying anymore. Had that horrible man taken RJ with him? No! As long as she had breath, she would do all she could to keep RJ from him and safe. She yanked and thrashed, pulling on the wrought-iron bar and the cuffs. Neither would budge. She stopped her flurry and stood motionless. There had to be a way out of this. The bolts. She tried to turn the bolts with her fingers. They remained tight. She shook the bar and tried again. Nothing.

Tears stung her eyes more from smoke than frustration. The pole was immovable as were the bolts. That left only the cuffs, and unlocking them was out of the question. The one around her right wrist was almost tight enough to cut off circulation. All that remained was the cuff around her left wrist, and there was only one way it would come off—even if she had to lose her hand to do it.

She pulled the cuff as far down on her hand as she could. Pressing her bones together and pulling her skin under the cuff, she moved the cuff across her bruises and further down her hand. She had heard of a woman in the Oklahoma City building bombing who had literally sacrificed her blood to keep her child alive. And she would do no less for hers.

The smoke was thickening, and she coughed. It was comforting to know the smoke would get her before the flames. She ground the cuff further down. The cuff was stuck on the lower thumb bone and knuckle bone of her little finger. She'd have to yank it, ripping her skin. She closed her eyes and took a deep breath and coughed out charred air. A sharp pain bit into her hand as she jerked on the cuff, but it was no closer to coming off. She ignored the pain and kept pulling. She wasn't strong enough to get the metal over the bones. She squeezed and pressed her hand bones as if dislocating them but without the added pain of dislocation. The cuff budged a little.

She coughed. The smoke at the ceiling crept lower and lower.

Roger had to go back in for Jackie. But how with RJ so determined to go in too? He scanned the area and saw a dumpster. He snatched RJ and ran. It was empty. Not ideal, but it would do. He lifted RJ inside. "You'll be safe here."

RJ cried harder.

Ignoring him, Roger sprinted toward the burning building. He ducked through the back doorway. It was hot inside. He wanted to shed his leather jacket but knew it would give him some degree of protection.

Sweeny had said she was upstairs. He covered his mouth and nose with his arm and dashed for the front where a staircase went up, into the heart of the inferno. Flames completely engulfed the staircase. No doubt all routes upstairs were cut off.

"Jackie!" His anguished call was eaten by the ferocious blaze. He backed away. There had to be another way up. He began to move. His feet seemed to know where to go even though he didn't.

Jackie lowered herself to the floor away from the thickest smoke. Kneeling caused the throbbing ache in her right calf to explode with shards of pain. She gritted her teeth and tried to control the pain with her breathing. She coughed. The room grew darker, warmer.

It was time to do something drastic. She'd have to break a bone to make her hand smaller. Could she do that to herself? If she were just a little stronger, she could pull her hand the rest of the way through, flesh or no flesh.

Strength! That was what she needed, and that was exactly what she had.

She lay on her back and propped one sneakered foot on each side of the cuff. *Lord, give me the inner strength to do this. Help me to endure the pain and not pass out.* She took a deep breath and held it, ignoring the urge to cough. One quick thrust with her legs and her hand was free. She cried out in pain and gripped it with her good hand, the cuff dangling from her wrist. It was slick and warm with blood. She rolled to her stomach and wriggled herself to her feet. RJ! She had to find RJ! She wouldn't leave without him.

❧

"Jackie!" Energized by Jackie's scream, Roger's feet moved him more quickly over the spongy floor. "Jackie!" He stayed to the wall and hoped the floor would hold him. "Jackie!" His throat burned, and it hurt to yell. She was alive, and he would call to her until she heard him. "Jackie!" Why wasn't she answering him? "Jackie!" He coughed. Did her scream indicate the fire had reached her? Was it her last gasp of life? "Jackie!"

❧

Jackie leaned on the door frame, put her arm over her mouth and nose, and hugged her bleeding hand. The hall was hotter and darker than the room. The smoke thickened, making her drowsy. She shook her head to clear it. She had to find RJ. She coughed, gagging on smoke.

Her head jerked up. What was that? Was RJ calling to her? No. He'd call "Mama." She hobbled across the hall and into the wall. She limped down the hall in the direction she had come. Or at least she thought she was moving.

❧

The heat inside the building made the rope burn on Roger's hand hurt more. He closed it into a fist. Jackie was here somewhere. But could he find her in time? Was it already too late. "Jackie!" He slid along the wall and around the corner, feeling his way down the hall to an open doorway. "Jackie!" He coughed and covered his mouth with his coat collar. The floor beneath him bowed and crackled. He found himself in the room with the rope. He grabbed the rope. The sting in his hand intensified. He jerked his hand back. "Jackie!"

&

That was her name! Roger was here and alive! "Roger!" She limped more quickly down the hall toward the smoke and heat. "Roger!"

She looked through the window of the fire door at the top of the stairwell. Flames licked up the stairs and at the door. They were all but gone. "Roger!"

"Jackie! Where are you?"

She coughed. "Here. Where are you? Where's RJ?"

"Follow my voice."

"I can't." It was so dark. She slunk to the floor on her knees and elbows. Roger must have RJ.

"Go to the apartment next to the stairs."

Next to the stairs? On which side?

"Follow my voice."

She tried crawling on her elbows but couldn't move very well. She relinquished her bleeding hand and did her best to crawl on one hand and her wrist. Ignoring the pain in her hand and her calf, she crawled along the wall to an open door. She hoped it was the right way.

"Are you there yet?"

She needed to rest but knew she couldn't. She had to keep going.

"Jackie!"

Roger's voice was closer. She had gone the right way. "Roger?" she choked out. "Are you in here?"

"Be careful—there's a hole in the floor."

"Where are you?"

"I'm down below. Find the edge of the hole."

She crawled across the floor to where she could feel it tip

down, dragging the cuff behind her right wrist. She moved around to the side where the floor sat level, and she could see a little. The smoke billowed up through the far side of the hole. She peered through. "Roger! Where's RJ?"

"He's outside. He's safe."

Roger seemed as relieved to see her as she was to hear RJ was safe. Roger had saved him. Her baby was safe.

"Grab this rope and climb down. Grab both ends of the rope at once."

She latched onto the ropes with her good hand, and her mind flashed back to seventh-grade PE class. She couldn't do this. She couldn't then, and she couldn't now. She'd nearly flunked PE.

"Climb down, Jackie!"

"I can't."

"Yes, you can."

The room began to turn. "No." She didn't do well with heights. Looking down through the hole made her dizzy. Or was it the smoke?

"Let go of the rope. I'm coming up."

"There has to be another way down."

"No time." He sent a ripple up the rope, and she let go. Roger leaped up the rope, ascending hand over hand.

Even with Roger, could she leave the floor and go down the hole? The floor seemed to shift, and with a crack and a crash something gave way. Falling debris rained down around Roger. A board struck him across the shoulders and knocked him to the floor.

"Roger!"

The rope swung back to her. She caught it without thinking and latched on with both hands. A bolt of pain shot up her wrist; but all she could think of was getting to Roger. Her injured hand was useless. She descended too quickly, burning her good hand. Part way down, her hand gave way, and she thumped to the floor. Pain exploded in her calf. She scooted to where Roger lay moaning, trying to move.

Roger slowly pushed to his hands and knees. "We have to get out of here before the whole place comes down on us."

In answer, another section of the ceiling crashed down. Jackie screamed, and Roger curled his body over hers.

fifteen

The force of the falling ceiling threw them to the floor, knocking the wind out of Jackie. She willed herself to draw in a gasp of air and coughed. She could feel the full weight of Roger's motionless body protecting her. "Roger?" Nothing. "Roger!"

Roger moaned.

"Roger, are you okay?"

He tried to move. "What?" He raised his weight off her. "We have to get out."

Lord, show us the way. She crawled free and helped him get out from under the debris. Jackie limped to the hall with Roger staggering beside her. She wasn't sure who was helping whom.

"This way." Roger steered them down the hall away from the heart of the fire.

She held her bloody hand against her stomach. "But the door—"

"—is eaten up in flames."

She gritted her teeth to stave off the pain in her calf. It didn't help.

At the end of the hall, they ducked through an open doorway. The smoke was thinner here away from the blaze. Roger dropped to his knees. "The window."

The window was jammed shut. With her less injured hand, she picked up a board to break it out. She swung, and glass crashed. She ran the board around the window frame to clear the glass. When she turned back around, Roger was lying on the floor. She ran to him and shook him, pulling him to a sitting position.

"Just go. I'll be along. I love you."

He couldn't really expect her to leave without him. "Not without you. I lost you for two and a half years. I'm not going to lose you again. Now get up!" She helped Roger to his feet and swung his arm across her shoulders. She could hardly bear her own weight let alone his too, but together they would make it—or not.

She helped him swing his leg out the window and put her hand on the back of his blood-matted hair to guide him through without bumping his head. He probably had a concussion. He rolled out and thumped to the ground. Jackie ignored the pain and swung her leg out and crawled through. She helped Roger across the wet grass and collapsed beside him. She took several deep breaths. The fresh air helped clear her head. Her lungs burned. She would need to be put on oxygen, as would Roger.

"Mah-mah-mah-mah." RJ's ragged crying cut through her fog.

She followed his small, raw voice to the dumpster.

"Sweetheart, Honey, here I am."

RJ looked up at her from the filthy floor. "Mah-mah, Mah-mah." His pleas became more frantic as he stood and stretched out his arms to her.

How was she going to lift him out with two injured hands? Her left hand was not only useless; the blood could scare RJ. She reached her burned hand in and grasped her son's upper arm. The dangling handcuff clanked against the side. She knew she shouldn't pull him up by one arm, but she had no other choice. "Climb, Honey—climb." She couldn't do this alone.

RJ grabbed two fistfuls of her bulky sweater sleeve and

scrambled up, desperate to get to her. He clutched her around the neck, making it easier for her to pull him the rest of the way out. She took a slow breath and coughed. Her son was safe.

She knelt back down next to Roger's still body. RJ wouldn't let loose of her so she had to examine Roger with RJ clinging to her. He had a gash on the back of his head that was still bleeding but not too badly. It was the concussion and smoke that worried her most, but she couldn't do anything about either of those at the moment. She gently separated his hair with one hand to get a better look at his laceration. A two-inch diagonal cut dripped blood. She needed to get Roger's head above his heart. Sitting in the wet grass, she tried to wiggle his head and shoulders onto her lap without luck.

Roger moaned and rocked his head to the side. "Ow!" His whole body tensed.

"Roger, can you sit up?"

"Sleep."

"No, you can't sleep. You have a concussion. I need you to sit up." She wrestled him into a sitting position against her with his help. She lifted one of his eyelids, then the other. Fixed and dilated. She took his pulse. Steady and strong.

"I'm so tired." His brain was fogged by a bruise and smoke.

"I know, but you can't go to sleep." How was she going to get him to a hospital? "Talk to me. What happened to that man who brought us here?"

"He got away."

"The CD?"

"That too."

"Oh, Roger." It was all her fault.

"It's okay. You and RJ are safe." Roger seemed to become more lucid the more he talked. The fresh air was helping them both.

Sirens whined in the distance. She willed them louder and closer. A portion of the building behind her crashed. A fire truck and rescue truck screamed to a stop. They'd be okay. Firemen rushed around, and two EMTs ran toward her.

"He has a concussion, pupils fixed and dilated. His pulse is strong and steady. He has a laceration on the back of his head, and he needs oxygen for smoke inhalation. We both do."

One EMT started on Roger. The other stared at her. "Are you a doctor?"

"Nurse."

"Is the boy hurt?"

"I don't think so. He wasn't in the building, but he should be checked."

A fireman rushed over. "We need to get these people farther away from the building." The fireman helped Roger up and over to the emergency vehicles. One EMT grabbed the medical equipment they had brought over, and the other one helped her and RJ. RJ wouldn't let the man carry him so the EMT supported and half carried her to safety.

They wrapped Roger's head and carefully strapped an oxygen mask to his face. They draped a blanket around Roger's shoulders and one around hers and gave her an oxygen mask to breath into.

Three police cars and a ladder truck pulled up. Two police officers came over. The officer with the name Stanley on his badge asked, "Are they okay? Can either of them talk?"

"Make it quick. I want to get them out of here as soon as the ambulance shows up."

"What were the two of you doing in a boarded-up condemned building?"

"A man kidnapped my son and me and brought us here. Roger came to rescue us." The air was damp and heavy, but it hadn't started to rain yet.

"Where is this man? Can you give us a description?"

Roger reached for the oxygen mask while the EMTs proceeded to remove his coat, with his coat sleeves and arms tangled together. They freed the coat. Roger finally managed to wrestle the mask off.

Suddenly both officers reached for their guns but didn't draw them. They stared at Roger, and the EMTs slowly moved back.

"Sir, we need your gun." Though Officer Stanley spoke calmly, there was authority behind his request.

Still dazed, Roger looked to his side. A brittle silence stretched out around the group, touching each one. Roger groped for his gun and pulled it out.

The officers tensed and remained ready to draw their weapons. "Easy, Sir."

Jackie moved her body in front of Roger, uprooting RJ next to her. She could feel the tension from the officers. They had no idea if Roger was a threat or not. "He has a concussion and isn't completely aware of his surroundings." She put one hand on top of Roger's and the gun. In his state, he could be thinking anything and mistake the officers as a threat. "Give me the gun."

Roger looked at her confused.

"Just give me the gun," she said gentler.

Roger looked her directly in the face. "I can do it."

Her only thought was trust, and she moved aside.

Roger kept his glazed eyes fixed on her as he stretched out his arm with his gun hanging from his index finger.

Officer Stanley took the gun. "Hope you have a permit for this."

"I do."

The officers relaxed, and everyone seemed to breathe more easily. The EMT who had latched onto RJ released him.

RJ ran back to her. "Chocoe? JJ good."

"Yes, I'll get you some chocolate."

"So that's what that means." Roger held out his arm for the EMT to wrap the blood pressure cuff on him.

"Can you tell me who this man was?" Officer Stanley pulled out a small key and unlocked the cuff still on her wrist. She wanted to rub her wrist, but Kevin, the EMT, was gently wrapping her other hand.

"I don't know his name. He was wearing a blue coat and pants and had short, curly, light brown hair."

"His name is Martin Sweeny. He's about five ten, a hundred and seventy pounds."

"Is he armed?"

"Not anymore right now. Lost his gun inside."

"What was he driving?"

Roger shook his head. "I don't know."

But she did. "A silver Ford Taurus, the license number is WSG 174."

"I'll put out an APB." Officer Stanley walked away.

RJ tugged on her arm. "JJ chocoe."

She looked up at Stanley's partner, Cardozo. "You wouldn't have a chocolate bar, would you?" It was worth a try.

"No, but Tom might." He left and returned a moment later with a crunchy chocolate bar. "Tom has a sweet tooth that won't end."

She thanked him, unwrapped the candy, and gave it to her son. He had braved the terror of Martin Sweeny and was already bouncing back.

An ambulance pulled up, and the EMTs lifted Roger onto a stretcher and loaded him into the back. "Aren't you coming?"

The first drop of rain hit Jackie's nose. "I'll catch the next bus." She could feel a portion of the tension drain away. They were away from this Martin Sweeny, and Roger was on his way to be treated.

"I don't want to let you out of my sight again."

She felt the same way. "I'll see you at the hospital." Another ambulance pulled up as Roger's drove away.

❧

"Where's my husband?" Jackie lay on the ER bed with an oxygen tube at her nose. No one would tell her anything. RJ wiggled and squirmed next to her. She'd never given him a whole chocolate bar before. He probably wouldn't nap until late and be cranky all day. One of the technicians had shown RJ how to use a tongue depressor, then gave it to him to play with. He had already checked her mouth a dozen times.

"Ma'am, just relax. The doctor will be with you soon." An ER nurse in panda-bear scrubs took her blood pressure and wrote it down.

"Can't you tell me anything about my husband? Where is he? Anything?"

"I'll see what I can find out." She swept around the curtain and tugged it shut behind her.

That nurse wasn't going to check on anything, Jackie told herself. It was a pat answer. Say whatever it took to keep a patient calm. She knew the game, and she didn't want to be placated. She wanted Roger!

A curtain separated her from the ER beds on either side of her. It was a thin veil of privacy, but right now it was too much. She wanted to throw back all the curtains so she could see what was going on in the whole ER.

After a few more mouth checks from RJ, the curtain was pulled back. "Hello, I'm Dr. Brown." And he was just that, a warm shade of brown with short, black hair, late thirties or forties. "How are you feeling?" He pulled up a rolling stool and sat down.

"Fine. A few scratches and a rope burn. I really don't know

why I'm in here." Only perhaps a half dozen reasons. But Roger was worse, and she wanted to check on him. These nurses wouldn't see to him as she would. And what if the doctor overlooked something? The nurse came back and waited for the doctor's orders.

"You have inhaled smoke, you're bleeding"—he pointed to her hand—"and your blood pressure is elevated. I would say 'fine' doesn't quite cover it."

"It's up because I'm agitated and anxious to get out of here and find my husband."

"Carol, would you check the waiting room for Mr. Villeroy?"

"I already did. He's not there."

"And why would he be? Or is it this hospital's policy to make a person who arrives in an ambulance wait in the reception area? He has a concussion and a laceration on his upper cranium, and he inhaled a lot of smoke."

"You a doctor?"

"Nurse. And I'm a good one."

"But not a very good patient. I thought that was reserved for us doctors." He wheeled himself beyond the curtain. "Paul, was a man with a head injury and smoke inhalation brought in by ambulance?"

"I think so."

"Where is he?"

"I don't know, but I'll find out."

"Thanks." Dr. Brown wheeled back. "The search is on. Now relax so we can take care of you." Nurse Carol unwrapped her bloody hand while the doctor examined her rope-burned hand. RJ proceeded to check her ears with the tongue depressor.

"Use a local on this and clean it well. Put on Silvaden and wrap it." The doctor circled to the other side of the bed. "How did you manage to scrape the skin off both sides of your hand? It looks as if you caught it in something."

"A handcuff."

"That one I haven't heard before. The bleeding has stopped but will start again when we clean it." Though he still examined her hand, she could tell he had switched from speaking to her to instructing the nurse. "Use a local. I'll have a look at it after it's clean and see if stitches will do any good."

She winced when he touched her little finger.

He raised his eyebrows at her.

"It may be broken." She didn't want to admit it because it would delay her from getting to Roger.

Though he didn't say anything, she could hear in her mind his earlier words, " 'fine' doesn't quite cover it." He scribbled his instructions on her chart and stood.

Paul came in then. "I found the missing patient, a Roger Villeroy, concussion and smoke. They stitched up his head. He's doing fine. They just moved him upstairs. Dr. Green wants to keep him overnight to be sure. And—he asked me to give you this." He pulled RJ's toy Harley from behind his back.

"Cycoe!" RJ dropped the stick and latched onto the toy. Now she would become a raceway.

"You can go up and see him when we get you patched up." The doctor's face broke into a broad smile.

It wouldn't be soon enough for her. She wanted to see Roger with her own eyes and determine if he was fine.

The doctor was about to say good-bye to her when he stopped. "What do we have here?" He frowned at her leg.

"A scratch?"

He gently lifted the hem of her jeans. "Your sock is soaked with blood, and you're bleeding on my bed. It's more than a scratch." He snatched up a pair of surgical scissors and cut her pants from the hem to the knee. "Paul, get me a warm, wet towel. Carol, get me a suture kit." Paul left, and Carol brought the kit.

By the time they'd finished fussing over her, she had called her parents, and Roger's doctor had paid her a visit to update her on his condition.

Dr. Brown left—seventeen stitches later. She hadn't realized her leg was so bad. She had been occupied with other things. Nurse Carol ordered her out of her clothes to check her for additional injuries. It wasn't easy getting dressed again with both her hands wrapped in a hundred pounds of gauze. They'd had a difficult time splinting and stitching her left hand.

The nurse wheeled her out with RJ on her lap. The doctor prescribed a wheelchair in addition to the amoxicillin and extra-strength pain reliever. He wanted her to stay off her leg for a few days, and with her hands injured, she couldn't use crutches.

Her parents were waiting for her. Her mother crossed to her first and scooped up RJ. "What did he do to you?"

Always the worst. "He saved our lives. Can we talk about it later? I want to go up and see Roger."

Her father took over the wheelchair from Carol. "The doctor said you should go home and rest."

"After I see Roger."

"We were so worried about you." Her father steered the chair toward the elevators.

"And when they found your van abandoned in a car wash—" Her mother had a vivid imagination and probably pictured the worst, but even she couldn't imagine all that had happened.

Her parents waited in the hall with RJ. She left the wheelchair by the door and hobbled in. She didn't want Roger to see her in it.

When she bumped into the bed, he opened his eyes. A smile stretched his mouth. "Are you my nurse?"

"No. I can't stay. I wanted to check on you before I go. How are you?"

"They put four staples in my head! What do they think—I'm a term paper?"

Jackie smiled, glad to see he hadn't lost his sense of humor. "The staples are better—trust me."

He reached for her hand and came up with a fistful of gauze. He gave her a sympathetic look. "I sure know how to show a girl a good time. All the best places."

"We're all safe. That's what matters."

"Thank the Lord." He raised her hand to his lips and kissed the tips of her fingers that were sticking out from the gauze.

A tingle swept through her body. She wanted to cuddle up next to him until the morning when she could take him home. But her parents were waiting, and she was drowsy from the long day and the morphine. "I have to go. I'll be back in the morning to take you home." Home. She liked the sound of that.

"I'll be counting the minutes."

She kissed him and hobbled away.

"Oh, before you go—they caught Sweeny. You don't have to worry."

She nodded and left. She would sleep easier knowing that man was behind bars.

❧

Roger lay awake, staring at the little holes in the ceiling panels and listening to the drone of activity from the hallway. He had slept most of the afternoon, lessening his chance for sleep tonight. Someone had come in with a dinner tray. He wasn't hungry. The fog in his head had cleared, and he was anxious to get out of there. Now that Sweeny was caught and the CD-ROM was, he hoped, in the right hands, the dominoes would begin to fall. He hoped he was left standing. It was out of his hands now and in the Lord's.

He wished Jackie would come back but knew she wouldn't until the morning. Maybe he should call her. Did she have a separate number? Would he have to talk to his in-laws? What if Jackie was asleep? He didn't want to wake her. She'd had a harrowing day.

They had a lot to talk about and decisions to make. Some decisions he might not like, but as long as Jackie was willing to work things out between them he could live with almost anything. She said she wanted to take him home. Whose home? He didn't have one, and she lived with her parents. But he wanted to be anywhere she was.

Startled by the phone, he swung around. A rush of pain flooded his head. He closed his eyes and took even breaths. He reached out where memory told him the phone was and picked up the receiver. "Hello."

"Did I wake you?" Jackie's lilting voice soothed away the remainder of the pain.

"You didn't wake me. I slept all afternoon. I was just thinking about you." He lay back on the bed. "In fact, I was considering calling you, but I don't have your number."

"Here, I'll give it to you."

He pulled a small tablet and half a pencil out of the nightstand drawer and wrote down the number. He lay back on the bed and closed his eyes, picturing Jackie's smiling face.

"I'm glad this is all over."

His gut tightened. "It may not be over yet."

"What do you mean? You said they caught the guy." He could hear the worry in her voice.

He didn't want to scare her, but he also wouldn't lie to her and tell her it was over. "This goes way beyond Sweeny. But no matter what happens, believe that the Lord will work everything out."

"What do you mean 'no matter what happens'? What else is going to happen?"

"I don't know. Maybe nothing concerning us. But I do know it'll all work out in the end. The Lord is in control of even this."

After an hour of letting Jackie's soothing voice wash over him, he relented and hung up.

He climbed out of bed and walked to the bathroom. He was supposed to call for help. He could make it on his own. When he came out, two men in suits were waiting for him. The Feds.

⋆

Jackie arrived at the hospital at a quarter to seven the next morning. Roger's release time was supposed to be seven. Her father drove her to the hospital and pushed her wheelchair through the halls. She would leave it in the hall again to go in to see him. What had Roger meant 'no matter what happens'? No more surprises. No more secrets.

As they neared Roger's room, two men in suits came out with Roger between them, his hands behind his back. "Jackie."

"Are you handcuffed?" She pushed herself out of the chair. "What's going on?" Her insides tightened.

"They have to take me in. It'll be fine."

"Fine? No! I don't want them to take you away." She wanted to take him away. This was what he meant by "no matter what happens." She looked at the two men. "You have the wrong guy. He hasn't done anything wrong."

Roger regained her attention. "Jackie. It'll be all right. I have a strange peace that makes no sense at all. Just trust God."

She put one gauze-wrapped hand on each side of his face

and kissed him. A tear rolled down her cheek as they took him away.

Lord, be with him. I trust You to get us all through this.

She felt a peace too. God was sufficient, no matter what happened.

Her father came up beside her and put a hand on her shoulder. "I'll take you home."

"I want to go wherever they are taking him."

"There's nothing you can do."

"I know, but it is better than sitting at home wondering."

He pulled the wheelchair up to her. "Then we'd better hurry."

sixteen

Jackie took each step slowly as she descended into the basement of the hospital, clutching the hand rail, her legs barely holding her weight. Could she do this again? The metal doors loomed before her with the word Morgue stamped in dark red letters. As she approached, ready to pass through the doors, the letters began to bleed. Beside the steel gurney, the sheet floated back. No, not Roger! "There's no mole." She looked around. "There's supposed to be a mole." She was alone in the cold room with the body. "Where's the mole?" No one was listening to her. "This isn't right."

Jackie bolted upright from her regular nightmare. It didn't come as often anymore. She and Roger in a burning building and she couldn't get him out, or he died at the hospital because they didn't think he was really hurt, or Martin Sweeny shot him. Sometimes it was all three. But they all ended with her a widow in the morgue.

She rolled toward Roger's side of the bed. Cold and empty. A moment of panic rippled through her. Roger couldn't be gone again. No, he was here, and this house was proof of it. ICOM Electronics had given him a sizable reward, ten percent of what he had saved them, for all the work he had done on their behalf. A mortgage-free house, four bedrooms, three baths, and a huge yard for RJ to play in along with all the brothers and sisters Roger planned for him to have.

Once everyone who would have wanted to harm them was behind bars, Roger explained to her that he'd had to go on the run from her to distance himself and the danger that pursued him. That he would come back to make sure she was indeed safe. He told her that Martin Sweeny had found out about her and RJ and threatened to harm them if Roger didn't cooperate. And when she had questions about his absence, and she had a lot, he answered her directly and fully, no more vague answers.

She wrapped her robe around herself and headed down the hall. RJ's bed was rumpled but empty. He was probably watching *Willie the Operatic Whale* for the seven hundredth time. Roger had some catching up to do in the children's video department. As she entered the kitchen, something in the dining room caught her eye. She walked three steps in reverse.

Four of the largest red roses she had ever seen sat in the middle of the table with four heart-shaped boxes of chocolates circling the vase. On each box was a different penguin, and each penguin held a helium balloon that said I love you on it. Beside the plethora of gifts was a note. She picked it up.

Happy Anniversary!
  One rose for each year. I love you with all my heart.
  RJ is at your parents'. Enjoy a quiet day to yourself.
  I made reservations at Manny's for 6:30. See you there.
                                        All my love,
                                            Roger

She read the card that had been hiding under the piece of paper. It echoed her own heart.

The rift between Roger and her parents was healing. They got along better now than ever. The long nights of talking things over had helped. Roger had been candid and honest with them. He told them about helping his friend Jim Moore, about Sweeny and the troubles with ICOM Electronics. Even her mother had warmed to him. She liked the idea of her son-in-law being a hero, though Roger flat out denied he was any kind of hero. Her mother had actually cooked his favorite food on his birthday last month, barbecued spare ribs. When Jackie had started to cry and Roger asked her about it, all she could do was squeak out the word happy.

A whole day to herself. She hadn't had a whole day to herself in a long time. What would she do? She could finish unpacking those boxes in the corner of the basement and make banana bread before the three bananas were too ripe. And the laundry always needed to be done.

But if Roger was leaving her to her own devices, she knew exactly how to spend her day—shopping! Top on her list was a dress to wow Roger, have her hair and nails done, get a facial. . . .

&

She almost bought a little red satin dress, but red wasn't her color. Instead she found a black velvet dress with faux diamond rhinestones, long sleeves, and a neckline that scooped just enough to show off the diamond cross necklace Roger had given her on their first anniversary. The piece de resistance was the back of the dress. In place of fabric a lattice work of faux diamonds was strung together.

She had thought about wearing a dumpy old dress or a faded T-shirt and holey jeans for leaving her alone all day on their anniversary. Two things stopped her. One, he'd remembered their anniversary. She recalled that her dad had been in the doghouse a number of times for forgetting. He'd tried to cover up with a hastily purchased card and a promise of a special dinner. Mom was never fooled. Two, she had spent almost enough money today to make up for his absence. But after her nightmare, she still felt that uneasiness of not seeing him and holding him. She couldn't wait.

First glimpse of the entrance to Manny's flashed her back

to the doors in her nightmare. She wished Roger was with her and not meeting her here. She took a deep breath and pulled the door open. Roger was not in the entrance waiting for her as she had expected.

The host approached her. "Right this way."

"I'm waiting for someone."

"Your table's ready."

She followed him. Roger must already be at the table. But how did the host know who she was?

"Your table." He pulled out a chair for her.

The same one. She sat down. She looked across the table at the empty chair. Where was Roger? Her breaths came in short, quick puffs. She could do this. Roger would be here. The chair almost seemed to push her out, but she willed herself to stay. She would trust Roger, but more important she would trust God. God had brought Roger back to her. She forced herself to take normal breaths, slow and even.

A waiter came and set a plate of grilled salmon, rice pilaf, and steamed vegetables in front of her. Across the table, he set a medium-well sirloin steak, baked potato with extra sour cream and chives on it, just the way Roger liked it, and the same kind of steamed vegetables. It was the very thing they had ordered last time. But she hadn't ordered. She didn't even have a menu yet. She turned to tell him so, but he was gone, and Roger was gazing down at her.

She jumped up to give him a hug as he leaned over, and she caught his chin with her shoulder. He grabbed his chin and mouth.

"Oh, Roger, I'm so sorry."

"Don't worry about it. I'm fine." His grimace contradicted that. "I don't want anything to spoil tonight."

She wrapped her arms, carefully this time, around Roger. She didn't care if people were staring. If they knew how long she had been waiting to spend just one anniversary with her husband, they would understand.

After they sat, Roger bowed his head and asked a blessing for their food, their anniversary, and a future filled with many more anniversaries together. She gave a hearty amen to that.

A cell phone rang at the next table. They both jumped, then laughed.

"No phones, no interruptions. Tonight is all ours." He lifted her hand to his lips and kissed it. "I wanted to pretend this was our first anniversary, but I want us to move forward into the future and not live in the past."

"I never want to relive our first anniversary." She lifted her water glass to him. He took her cue. "To the future."

"The future." He clanked his glass against hers.

She sipped the water and set her glass down then turned as four men in white shirts and red bow ties approached their table. One man put a small metal thing to his mouth and blew. A tone like that of a harmonica came out, and all four men hummed.

"Let me call you sweetheart. I'm in love with you," they sang in perfect four-part harmony.

Roger reached across the table and took her hand. She gave his a squeeze, listening to every word of her serenade.

When the quartet had left, Roger came around the table and kissed her. "I have been wanting to do that since I saw you get out of the van." He sat back down. "And there is more where that came from when we get home."

She felt suddenly warm.

The waiter interrupted then. "Is everything to your liking?"

"Just fine," Roger said with a lopsided grin.

The waiter turned to her.

She kept her gaze locked with Roger's when she spoke to the waiter. "Could we get these to go?"

A Letter To Our Readers

Dear Reader:

In order that we might better contribute to your reading enjoyment, we would appreciate your taking a few minutes to respond to the following questions. We welcome your comments and read each form and letter we receive. When completed, please return to the following:

Rebecca Germany, Fiction Editor
Heartsong Presents
PO Box 719
Uhrichsville, Ohio 44683

1. Did you enjoy reading *Roger's Return* by Mary Davis?
   ❑ Very much! I would like to see more books by this author!
   ❑ Moderately. I would have enjoyed it more if

   _____

   _____

   _____

2. Are you a member of **Heartsong Presents**? ❑ Yes ❑ No
   If no, where did you purchase this book? _____

   _____

3. How would you rate, on a scale from 1 (poor) to 5 (superior),
   the cover design? _____

4. On a scale from 1 (poor) to 10 (superior), please rate the
   following elements.

   ____ Heroine   ____ Plot
   ____ Hero   ____ Inspirational theme
   ____ Setting   ____ Secondary characters

6. How has this book inspired your life?_____
_____
_____

7. What settings would you like to see covered in future
   Heartsong Presents books? _____
_____
_____

8. What are some inspirational themes you would like to see
   treated in future books? _____
_____
_____

9. Would you be interested in reading other **Heartsong
   Presents** titles? ❏ Yes ❏ No

10. Please check your age range:
    ❏ Under 18   ❏ 18-24
    ❏ 25-34   ❏ 35-45
    ❏ 46-55   ❏ Over 55

Name_____
Occupation _____
Address _____
City_____ State_____ Zip_____
E-mail_____

SEATTLE

Shepherd of Love Hospital stands as a beacon of hope in Seattle, Washington. Its Christian staff members work with each other—and with God—to care for the sick and injured. But sometimes they find their own lives in need of a healing touch.

Can those who heal find healing for their own souls? How will the Shepherd for whom their hospital is named reveal the love each one longs for?

Contemporary, paperback, 480 pages, 5 ³⁄₁₆" x 8"

❤ ❤ ❤ ❤ ❤ ❤ ❤ ❤ ❤ ❤ ❤ ❤ ❤ ❤ ❤ ❤ ❤

❤ ❤ ❤ ❤ ❤ ❤ ❤ ❤ ❤ ❤ ❤ ❤ ❤ ❤ ❤ ❤ ❤

Heartsong

Any 12 Heartsong Presents titles for only $30.00*

CONTEMPORARY ROMANCE IS CHEAPER BY THE DOZEN!

Buy any assortment of twelve *Heartsong Presents* titles and save 25% off of the already discounted price of $3.25 each!

*plus $2.00 shipping and handling per order and sales tax where applicable.

HEARTSONG PRESENTS TITLES AVAILABLE NOW:

__HP177 *Nepali Noon,* S. Hayden	__HP318 *Born for This Love,* B. Bancroft
__HP178 *Eagles for Anna,* C. Runyon	__HP321 *Fortress of Love,* M. Panagiotopoulos
__HP181 *Retreat to Love,* N. Rue	__HP322 *Country Charm,* D. Mills
__HP182 *A Wing and a Prayer,* T. Peterson	__HP325 *Gone Camping,* G. Sattler
__HP186 *Wings Like Eagles,* T. Peterson	__HP326 *A Tender Melody,* B. L. Etchison
__HP189 *A Kindled Spark,* C. Reece	__HP329 *Meet My Sister, Tess,* K. Billerbeck
__HP193 *Compassionate Love,* A. Bell	__HP330 *Dreaming of Castles,* G. G. Martin
__HP194 *Wait for the Morning,* K. Baez	__HP337 *Ozark Sunrise,* H. Alexander
__HP197 *Eagle Pilot,* J. Stengl	__HP338 *Somewhere a Rainbow,* Y. Lehman
__HP205 *A Question of Balance,* V. B. Jones	__HP341 *It Only Takes a Spark,* P. K. Tracy
__HP206 *Politically Correct,* K. Cornelius	__HP342 *The Haven of Rest,* A. Boeshaar
__HP210 *The Fruit of Her Hands,* J. Orcutt	__HP346 *Double Take,* T. Fowler
__HP213 *Picture of Love,* T. H. Murray	__HP349 *Wild Tiger Wind,* G. Buck
__HP217 *Odyssey of Love,* M. Panagiotopoulos	__HP350 *Race for the Roses,* L. Snelling
	__HP353 *Ice Castle,* J. Livingston
__HP218 *Hawaiian Heartbeat,* Y.Lehman	__HP354 *Finding Courtney,* B. L. Etchison
__HP221 *Thief of My Heart,* C. Bach	__HP358 *At Arm's Length,* G. Sattler
__HP222 *Finally, Love,* J. Stengl	__HP361 *The Name Game,* M. G. Chapman
__HP225 *A Rose Is a Rose,* R. R. Jones	__HP366 *To Galilee with Love,* E. M. Berger
__HP226 *Wings of the Dawn,* T. Peterson	__HP377 *Come Home to My Heart,* J. A. Grote
__HP234 *Glowing Embers,* C. L. Reece	__HP378 *The Landlord Takes a Bride,* K. Billerbeck
__HP242 *Far Above Rubies,* B. Melby & C. Wienke	__HP390 *Love Abounds,* A. Bell
__HP245 *Crossroads,* T. and J. Peterson	__HP394 *Equestrian Charm,* D. Mills
__HP246 *Brianna's Pardon,* G. Clover	__HP401 *Castle in the Clouds,* A. Boeshaar
__HP261 *Race of Love,* M. Panagiotopoulos	__HP402 *Secret Ballot,* Y. Lehman
__HP262 *Heaven's Child,* G. Fields	__HP405 *The Wife Degree,* A. Ford
__HP265 *Hearth of Fire,* C. L. Reece	__HP406 *Almost Twins,* G. Sattler
__HP278 *Elizabeth's Choice,* L. Lyle	__HP409 *A Living Soul,* H. Alexander
__HP298 *A Sense of Belonging,* T. Fowler	__HP410 *The Color of Love,* D. Mills
__HP302 *Seasons,* G. G. Martin	__HP413 *Remnant of Victory,* J. Odell
__HP305 *Call of the Mountain,* Y. Lehman	__HP414 *The Sea Beckons,* B. L. Etchison
__HP306 *Piano Lessons,* G. Sattler	__HP417 *From Russia with Love,* C. Coble
__HP317 *Love Remembered,* A. Bell	__HP418 *Yesteryear,* G. Brandt

(If ordering from this page, please remember to include it with the order form.)

Presents

Great Inspirational Romance at a Great Price!

Heartsong Presents books are inspirational romances in contemporary and historical settings, designed to give you an enjoyable, spirit-lifting reading experience. You can choose wonderfully written titles from some of today's best authors like Hannah Alexander, Andrea Boeshaar, Yvonne Lehman, Tracie Peterson, and many others.

When ordering quantities less than twelve, above titles are $3.25 each.
Not all titles may be available at time of order.

SEND TO: **Heartsong Presents** Reader's Service
P.O. Box 721, Uhrichsville, Ohio 44683

Please send me the items checked above. I am enclosing $ _____
(please add $2.00 to cover postage per order. OH add 6.25% tax. NJ add 6%.). Send check or money order, no cash or C.O.D.s, please.

To place a credit card order, call 1-800-847-8270.

NAME _____

ADDRESS _____

CITY/STATE _____ ZIP_____

HPS 13-02

*H*EARTSONG ❤ PRESENTS

Love Stories
Are Rated G!

That's for godly, gratifying, and of course, great! If you love a thrilling love story but don't appreciate the sordidness of some popular paperback romances, **Heartsong Presents** is for you. In fact, **Heartsong Presents** is the only inspirational romance book club featuring love stories where Christian faith is the primary ingredient in a marriage relationship.

Sign up today to receive your first set of four, never-before-published Christian romances. Send no money now; you will receive a bill with the first shipment. You may cancel at any time without obligation, and if you aren't completely satisfied with any selection, you may return the books for an immediate refund!

Imagine. . .four new romances every four weeks—two historical, two contemporary—with men and women like you who long to meet the one God has chosen as the love of their lives. . .all for the low price of $10.99 postpaid.

To join, simply complete the coupon below and mail to the address provided. **Heartsong Presents** romances are rated G for another reason: They'll arrive Godspeed!